JAMES
BUFFALO

& A FIT OF BAD DHARMA

James Buffalo
&
A Fit of Bad Dharma

A Novel
by
Nigel Schroeder

TIRED COAST PUBLISHING

James Buffalo & A Fit Of Bad Dharma

TIRED COAST PUBLISHING
San Diego, California

Library of Congress Catalog Card Number:
ISBN-13: 978-0692885277
ISBN-10: 0692885277

Printed in the United States of America

To my grandfather, Johann Schroeder.
I promise to be great.

PROLOGUE

I fell in love with the world when I was a child. I fell in love with a woman when I became a man. And when I became an intellectual, I fell in love with my own mind. Somewhere in my quest for the everlasting Dharma, all three of these loves escaped me. By all means, this is a love story.

CHAPTER
—1—

Mary Ann Lewis ran onto the elevator out of breath and late for work. Stephen Chauncey flinched as the elevator doors closed. I bit my lip, wrestled my collar, and promised myself I'd quit smoking.

As we ascended, cold sweat leaked from my brow. I was certain I reeked of Camel Golds. Tight spaces made me somewhat ashamed of this habit. As Mary Ann Lewis struggled to catch her breath, I dared not move.

On the seventh floor, Mary Ann Lewis would leave me. When she left, I would carry on with Steve to the tenth floor, where he would exit. I would eventually depart on the eleventh floor. That was the routine.

I closed my eyes in anticipation and waited as we passed the sixth floor. "Ding-Ding!" shouted the elevator. Good-bye, Mary Ann Lewis.

I felt the fleeting urge to grab her arm as she left. Run, Mary Ann Lewis. *Run with me*, I thought. I am bolder with each drawn breath. Together we could stretch across the state lines in a blur, tasting the salt of

California, Oregon, and Washington. With the windows down, your blonde hair would catch in the wind as if it had always meant to be in motion, dancing effortlessly and streaking across your face like stars falling from a tormented October sky. Together we could be free. You'd smile, and I'd wave to the long-haired children occupying the coastal towns. I'd loosely take the wheel of my van, guiding us in no particular direction except up and through. Up and through the sweet-smelling California pines. The native trees would dance along the highway as we sped past—two mad lovers with not a care in the world. And as the pines moved their limbs rhythmically in the wind, pine needles would spiral down and collect on the windshield like snow, and sunlight would splash across our faces like loose acrylic. Together, Mary Ann Lewis, we could taste heaven's paintbrush.

Imagining these wonderful things was exhausting. I grasped and hung to the railing as the elevator jerked upward past the sixth floor. I did my best to enjoy every warm detail until I felt nothing at all—my lust and big dreams abandoned like a bowl of lukewarm cereal.

I would have to return to that thought later. So, reluctantly, I pushed the winding coastal roads and time well spent with Mary Ann Lewis to the back of my mind. I closed my eyes with the concentrated fear that rational thinking would leave me unraveled and alone in the void.

Clutter. It is all clutter, I thought. There must be cleanliness. The horizon was clear and glowing—yes, no fighter jets, no battleships, and no explosive reclusion into deep thinking. I needed a swift passage into the present. My mind was an ocean, my body her loyal vessel. And I must do the right things to keep my vessel clean and sharp.

"Woo-hoo-hoo-hhheee! That Mary Ann is a real firecracker," Steve whispered as he planted a playful punch in my unsettled stomach.

"Good evening, Stevie. Please don't touch me," I replied, failing to make eye contact with the burly, red-haired man. "And she likes to be called Mary Ann Lewis, not Mary Ann."

"Oh please, you don't know that," snapped Steve. I watched as he smirked and nervously fiddled with the knot of his tie. "And I prefer to be called Steve," he said. "I am no longer a child."

I ignored his request and turned my attention to a button that had come loose on the sleeve of my shirt. A faded denim shirt I adored because of its weathered appearance. I had pulled it off a drifter at the Del Mar Race Track. The blond, heavyset man assured me of its quality, relenting that he must part ways with it due to some "stuck luck." I gave him seven dollars for the long-sleeved denim and watched as he instantly placed five dollars on a horse named Sal's Salvation to win in the seventh race. His broad jaw crooked up, and he looked back at me with a devilish smirk.

"Always bet the nines," he said. And he said this with such confidence and such ease I knew it must be true. I also knew that it didn't really matter, as he spent the remaining two dollars on a draft beer.

Sal's Salvation ended up winning by more than three lengths despite forty-eight-to-one odds. Sometime during the race, when the ponies were kicking dirt, it hit me that Sal's Salvation must be a reference to Sal Paradise, my favorite character from my favorite novel, *On the Road*. And afterward, when the results were official, I watched as the shirtless man disappeared from the trackside railing and into the crowd. I tried to catch up with him. I pushed and shoved, but the human doors closed, and a strange feeling of loss came over me as if I had just watched America's last baseball slide into a sewer drain. I needed to know *why*. I needed to know if he knew about Sal Paradise, and I needed to know of all the marvelous things he once held in the depths of the twin breast pockets I so proudly wore on my chest that day. Hell, I needed to be *that man*—free, unencumbered, and wonderfully reckless.

With the button securely in its place, I looked up and turned toward Steve, my unwanted companion. For the next two floors he would proceed to inform me of all the *things he would do* to Mary Ann Lewis if given the chance. I would do my best not to vomit, my collar growing increasingly tight with each crude remark. Strangely, I felt compelled to smile and nod. As Steve pumped anxiety into my flesh, I generously produced fraudulent yet passable laughter. I wondered if Mary Ann Lewis was conscious of her transcendence through the minds of those shallow and deep. I supposed it did not matter.

I would catch my breath in between the ninth and tenth floors as Steve would complete his evening ritual with the straightening of his tie and a hopeful glance toward his phone before powering it down. I had heard the doctors don't like it when your phone goes off during a session.

"Ding-Ding!" shouted the elevator again.

"Good-bye, *Stevie*," I said as he stepped out.

"Kick rocks, James!" he whispered all nasty, his face turning bright red, the same color as his hair and dumb freckles. I laughed to myself as the elevator doors closed in his burning face, and I kept laughing until I reached the eleventh floor. It was my turn to exit. "Ding-Ding!" I pulled my body between the metal doors and proceeded into the brightly lit hallway.

Thirty-six paces. That was the distance between the Doctor's office and the elevator landing.

After four paces, I passed the friendly receptionist, Clarence Beverly, a middle-aged black woman with three children: Christine, Marcus, and I had forgotten the third child's name. With the phone to her ear and the cord tangled in between her bare ring finger and middle finger, she motioned a loving hello.

Seven paces later, I stood before the coffee-break room. I turned to my right and shined a bright smile toward the white suits as they poured life into mugs that read the world's corniest sayings. Swiftly I turned away and continued walking.

Nine paces all to my lonesome. I hummed and sang to myself. I pretended to kick a stone down the grim hallway, oblivious to the sickly nature of things around there. I used to kick the stone with Doris. In the hallway, with my eyes closed, I could taste the air of a better day. I became a six-year-old child again. And it was my first real day of school. I was dressed in a jean jacket and matching jean overalls of Doris's choosing, and I was nervous, as rain fell and ran in torrents down the cobblestone driveway.

I asked Doris to walk alone, though I didn't really want to. "We'll walk through the park" she had said, "to save some time." Her skinny hand grabbed mine, and with a tug she practically catapulted me off the porch. The rain fell harder, and the denim got heavy on my back as we walked toward the park. My yellow rain boots kicked a pinecone down the water-covered path, and I started to feel a little less nervous as Doris, my champion, joined in. "Just think," she said, as I really gave the pinecone a wallop, "in a few years you will be the one walking Eli to school."

I miss the rain.

I miss the way everything smells afterward, so clean and so fresh, as if the sins of the world have been washed away. I miss the damp smell of childhood.

Back in the brightly lit hallway, I pushed a hand through my hair and smiled as Jody, the mail girl, pretended to kick the stone to me. Jody Eloise had two first names. She also had the softest eyes I had ever seen on a woman of twenty years of age. A slender frame, skinny elbows, and fine brown hair much like my own. She often made longing eyes at me.

I had spent many hours watching her push the overstocked mail cart down the hallway, clinging desperately onto the envelopes and brown paper packages that sought to escape her grasp. The slightest ripple in the carpet sent the day's incomings across the floor. Nice girl.

Sixteen more paces. I was outside of Doctor Henry P. Whitehouse's corner office. I liked the Doctor. Or I should say, I liked the pills he gave me. The pills helped me forget sad things, or at least I thought they did. I don't remember. *Kidding.*

At first glance, I thought the Doctor to be devastatingly interesting, which admittedly he was. However, upon further examination, I found him sick with a more common cruelty. His eccentric behavior seemed to mask something darker. I was sure he had secrets and I liked him for this. And before I found some sort of *Better Dharma*, I was very much in love with his methods for curing a complexity of nervousness that had become me.

With my hand pressed on the doorknob, I suddenly realized in an unforeseen panic that I had reached my destination. I retraced my steps—elevator landing, the reception desk with Clarence Beverly, the coffee-break room with the corny mugs, the brightly lit hallway with Jody Eloise, and there I stood, thirty-six paces exactly. The Doctor's pills always came at a price.

I wanted to leave; like a coward I wanted to run. *I'll take the stairs!* I thought to myself. Yes, Clarence will cover for me. She must! I turned back toward the exit, and I saw a tall, hunkering figure rounding the opposite corner in front of the stairs. His head was down, and a curved baseball cap covered his face. The man was Bruno Casey, and I knew my plans to leave were foiled. Bruno was a bloodthirsty drunk brought into counseling after beating a few cops pretty good. He was always asking if I wanted to get drunk and make fun of the "fags in suits" at the local Denny's. I hated Bruno, even more than I disliked Steve and his shrewd comments about Mary Ann Lewis—my plans were truly cooked. With a calamity of nervousness I fell into the Doctor's office, my hip jarring on the sharp metal handle, before Bruno could detect my presence.

The smell of burning incense made me aware of my surroundings.

"You look flush, James," the Doctor said.

I had no desire to mention to the Doctor my qualms with Bruno in that night's session, so I ignored the comment.

"Have you seen today's *Herald West*?" I diverted as the old man stood near the window with his back to me. He was looking out over the blossoming metropolitan night. He motioned for me to enter, and I closed the door.

I noticed the *Herald West* was folded neatly across his desk.

The Doctor, in his old age, still held some great stature. His hair was grey but showed no signs of recession, and his beard was full and primarily black, slightly grey at the tips, like snow on a summer mountain. Doctor Henry P. Whitehouse wasn't as tall as he used to be. However, time had given him an overabundance of confidence, and he could still make a younger man feel small when he wanted. The man dressed as if he were the captain of some great ship, and he very well may have been at one point in his life. That night, the old man was wearing a navy blue sailing coat. The jacket was cut perfectly to fit his skinny frame, tight around his long arms, fashioned with small gold buttons on the chest and sleeves.

"Would you like a drink, James?" the Doctor asked as he motioned lazily toward a bottle of Crown Royal on his desk. He was still standing with his back to me, surveying the lights of the young night.

"I don't think it's appropriate," I said, taken aback by the offering. Truthfully, I was already a little drunk anyway.

"Tea it is! You like tea, James, and that is good, and that is fine!" cried the Doctor. He turned away from the window and began to pace the room as if the patterned carpet burned his feet. "Please sit," he said stroking the grey tip of his beard. "I'm sorry for the dramatic nature of things this evening."

I watched as the Doctor walked to the side of the room and proceeded to light the pellet stove, placing a pot of tea above the flame. He carried himself in an aged and elegant manner that can only be obtained through the indulgence of truly living. His office reflected this weathered grandeur. The chair I sat in was made of flush maroon leather, fashioned with bronze rivets. To my left, there was a cluttered bookshelf that housed an obscure collection of readings. It was completely functional yet leaning slightly to the right, a product of the Doctor's drunken carpentry. Next to the slanted bookshelf, there was a stone fireplace, which was unlit. Above where the fire would have been, there was a painted mural of the Doctor standing next to a small horse. I considered this painting rather absurd.

I noticed the walls were draped with one of the Doctor's more eccentric wallpapers. The newly applied wallpaper was tan in its base and primarily covered with spiraling green vines. The Doctor had a fancy for changing the color of his walls once every few weeks or so. A habit that I fully understood—a habit that drove the assistants responsible for applying the Doctor's most recent taste in décor to the brink of insanity, as if his mere presence in their lives hadn't already done so.

"Dutchman's pipe, James," injected the Doctor, who reclined lazily behind his desk. I watched as he tossed his feet upon his cluttered work place, his white leather boat shoes sending an assortment of colored pens to the floor. Seemingly he did not notice this transgression, and writhing in his madness, he stared at me with the crazed look of a psychopath.

"Well, go on. Tell me, Dutchman's pipe!" He said again with enthusiasm. I shook my head, clearly confused. He then leaned across his desk and whispered, "What do you think of the walls?"

I thought for a moment and looked over the vine-covered wallpaper again. "I think if you change these damn walls one more time your lovely assistant Heather may just kill you!" And with that we laughed like schoolchildren as the teapot's cries went unnoticed.

As our laughter ceased, the teapot's screams became audible, and the Doctor poured two cups of green tea into the designated china. I watched as the steam billowed from the small teacups the Doctor had placed at opposite ends of his desk. I wanted to feel the sensation of the warm liquid crawling down my throat and into my stomach. I wanted to be warmed so badly. So, I reached toward the cup, took a healthy sip, and promptly burnt my tongue.

The Doctor, a man of movement, had begun to frantically pace before one of his pharmaceutical cabinets that stood beside the tilted bookshelf. I watched as the old man began to ravage through the drawers, finally removing a familiar purple pharmaceutical bottle labeled MRX2857.

Spinning toward me and opening the capsule in one fluid motion, the Doctor smiled and said, "It's clutter; it's all clutter, James." The old man cleared his throat. "No clutter as tomorrow becomes today. Do you agree?"

"Yes." I replied, and the Doctor poured three pills onto the table. "No clutter as tomorrow becomes today." The tea was cooler, and it did not burn as I swallowed the modern medicine.

I was exhausted, and I handed the Doctor some notes I had taken on the bus, hoping to fast-track the process. I had to rest, and I assumed the Doctor had work to do. I was right, but he insisted we talk a bit before I left.

"So, how was your energy today?" He asked me, speaking in a more serious tone. He had pulled my file from his desk and sat in an upright position of authority.

My heart sank a bit as I battled the evening's mood shifts.

"I suppose my energy was fine—it's all right there in my notes," I replied, crossing my legs and facing the Doctor. He slid his wired spectacles upon his face and opened the notes I had given him. I wanted to tell him

I felt like a ghost; however, I refrained, unsure of how a ghost should feel.

"Cmmm—good," coughed the Doctor as he reached to the spot on his desk where his pens should be. I uncrossed my legs and handed the Doctor one of the ink pens that had fallen to the floor earlier, unsure of its color. "And how are we applying this newfound energy, James? Toward living, I hope!"

"Yes, of course," I replied quickly, watching my tone, making sure it was credible.

"You know we have to talk, and these notes are, well...," the Doctor said as he examined the leather journal in his hands, flipping through a few pages before handing it back to me. "They're, uh, well...," he paused for a second. "They're a good idea," he continued. "However, we have to talk—you know that. It's a part of the agreement. I can't just give you medication without conversing with you for a bit."

I pushed the journal back across the desk toward the Doctor, and the old man chuckled. "Tell me, James, what are your plans for moving forward from this very moment right here?" he said.

I told the Doctor all I wanted to do was take care of my body. "Do the right things, you know?"

I knew, and he knew, that I had said this many times before. Then I went and did the opposite and got my wires all good and twisted, my connection to the holy land of good things all gone and lost. Still, I told the old kook I didn't care about all the pretty women in the world anymore.

"I don't want to fuck anyone!" I would exclaim, reciting a verse from the Diamond Sutra on celibacy. He would pretend to buy it, and I would secretly think in my head, *Yeah, I don't want to fuck anyone. What laughs! I don't want to fuck anyone except Mary Ann Lewis and Jody Eloise!*

I was still very much in practice with the *Bad Dharma*. I was doing and thinking bad things in an effort to find better things, and still I wanted something more. So I'd tell the old man I just wanted to be inside myself again. And I'd tell him I just wanted to feel like a child. I wasn't sure if I meant these words, though I really wished I did.

I would check out for the rest of the session, take a mental vacation, before things got too personal and my palms started to sweat. I was willing to submit my mind to the old man as long as I could avoid feeling naked. The medication was working, and I wished for a moment that I was a better man, a stronger man, but everything seemed so hard and dull, sharp and dangerous without the pills. So I would answer the Doctor's questions in such a manner that would provide a fitting ending to his inquiries with little personal exposure. The Doctor would receive the answers he knew he should, and I would derive satisfaction from this, my tail wagging like a Labrador as he patted my head.

Assured my departure in spirit would go undetected, I calmly drew a sip from the teacup, which was no longer emitting warmth to my lips, and started to answer the Doctor's questions. I could feel my heart rate slow as the questions began to feel less and less personal. Eventually I became a spectator, a fly on the ever-changing walls of Doctor Henry P. Whitehouse's corner office.

I didn't know much about the medication the Doctor had prescribed me. The old man had told me it was a high-grade antidepressant of sorts. I guessed it was working because the Doctor told me that night I was improving. I could see myself sitting cross-legged in the maroon chair. The Doctor turned on his desk lamp and killed the brighter ceiling lights. I imagined the dim lighting made me look handsome. I started to relax my eyes. My eyes felt so tired, yet they held no shame as I spilled the scary secret details of my mind.

Doctor Henry P. Whitehouse seemed happy. His hands blurred together as he rapidly recorded our conversation in his journal. I was happy, too. When the examination came to an end, the Doctor handed me two weeks' worth of MRX2857 and told me to see him in such time. I nodded, feeling refreshed and pleasantly lightheaded. I finished my tea and completed the remaining thirty-six paces back to the elevator. I was looking forward to having a good smoke.

CHAPTER
— 2 —

I emerged beneath the soft street lamps without a care in the universe. The air was cool and I could smell a fire burning in the park. I imagined the park bums huddled together sharing stories. Passing around a bottle, heads turned toward the sky in mad laughter. The sky was truly beautiful, and I took time to notice it for myself. I am not big on constellations. However, I was sure I could see them all. For all the things going wrong in America, it sure did have a beautiful ceiling.

I lit a cigarette and strolled to the corner of Elm and Market. It was around nine o'clock, and the evening crowds were beginning to gather outside of the bars and restaurants. Street musicians played their hearts out wailing on guitars and makeshift drums. They were the true soul of the city, and they knew it.

Every time I came into the city, I made sure to visit a street man by the name of Charlie. He reminded me of one of those Dharma bums I had read about, though he never seemed to practice Buddhism. He just seemed to have some sort of understanding, an understanding that is very hard to explain. The type of understanding every good mother wishes upon her child, the understanding a kitten has when it dips its tongue into warm milk for the first time, the understanding that there is nothing to want that you don't already have, the understanding that it's just your own feet moving on asphalt, a type of understanding that comes with great movement through sad cities. A man without a home, Charlie had paid his dues with currency of the heart.

No one knew his last name. And old Charlie claimed to have played in Edward Sharpe and the Magnetic Zeros before the release of their hit single "Home." He said he hated the song and that was the reason he left the band. Everyone knew Charlie was never in the band; however, Charlie wouldn't give it up. "I'll tell ya, man, I saaay right der thasss the problaam," he'd say. "Disss sonnggg gonnna appeaalll tooo the massesss and theyyy gonnnnnna go get gone and eat it up. Whilllleeee we on stage servin' it up, they gonnnaaaa keep eatin! Annn' before we knows it they gonnnna eat us, man! Eventually the preseedent gonna get hungry too and he come now and play our song all the time up in his beeeg white house. He gonnnaaa play it while he's makin love to the missis! He gonnnna play it while he's takin a bath just scrubin' and lisssnenn to our song! Jus scrubbin' and lisssnenn to our song! Washin' away all dat oil on his body, laughin' as they drill Alaskah! Singin' dem der words we wrote and he don't knowwwaaa damn 'bout wat it is we sayin down here. It's gonnna be ova for me and you right there! I sayy we aint never gonnna get our souls back after that, man."

I had been trying to get Charlie off the streets for years, but he insisted his soul belonged "amongst the people." I was never really sure what he meant by that.

I had offered him a nice bed in a nice home, but he just scoffed, saying, "Pleaseee, maaan, you dun know I live in thaa mos' beautiful home in the world, and you standin' in it! Whatchya feet on Gawd's carpet now!"

I told him that I had hoped his home had heat because it was going to be the coldest winter the Tired Coast had ever seen. And I wasn't "*keedddinn.*" It was only early December and the temperature was already forty-five degrees. "That Dharma blanket of yours isn't going to keep your old bones warm," I'd yell, and he would just laugh and shake his head and say, "No, but the wine will." I wondered where old Charlie was right then and went down to Peterson's Liquor, his usual hangout. Peterson's Liquor was a popular hangout for coast bums, and you could usually find Charlie out back playing *cee-lo* for cigarettes. The owner, Hank Peterson, was a good man and could often be found drinking with the street crowd outside of his store. I had planned on buying Charlie a few drinks just to warm him up, and I wanted to see Hank as well.

I crossed Main Street in a hurry, excited by the prospect of good conversation. A rush of yellow flashed in front of me as I stepped off the curb. I had almost collided with a taxi full of older broads. The driver laid on the horn and gave me the finger. I smiled and lowered my cigarette as a woman dressed in red reached her head out the rear window and whistled, "It'd be a damn shame to waste such a pretty face crossing Main Street, honey."

Taking the woman's advice, I safely crossed the street, turning my gaze toward the liquor store's neon pink sign that flickered seductively in the night. I approached the glowing storefront and circled around back, certain Charlie was caught in the middle of a thrilling dice game. However, my excitement was not met, as the back alley was deserted except for the presence of a few stray cats. Damn. I looped back around front, took one last drag, and carefully extinguished my fag before tossing it into a nearby trash can. I hated smokers, especially smokers who walked around treating the world as their own personal ashtray.

"James!" Hank shouted merrily as I entered the store. I tried not to laugh as I saw the heavyset man atop a rolling ladder. He was attempting to restock a half-drunk bottle of Jameson.

I chuckled. "Sure you got the right bottle, Hank?"

My bearded friend looked down at the half-gone fifth in his hand and burst into joyous laughter. "Ahh-haaahh shit, man, whaddda night," the big man slurred as he jumped off the ladder, sending it sliding halfway across the liquor rack. At that point, I was fully gone off the Doctor's prescription and buzzing nicely off the tobacco as well. I wasn't angry or depressed; I was simply content with whatever was to come. So when Hank poured three shots on the counter, I didn't object. Before we tasted the liquor, Hank hurried to the backroom and placed a vinyl on his old record player.

My companion grinned. "Cheers, buddy."

I could make out Buffalo Springfield's self-titled album scratching from the back, Hank's favorite. I raised my shot glass, which had a cartoon drawing of two pigs fucking, and slid the liquid down my throat. My stomach began to burn, and I laughed as Hank downed the other two shots.

Hank tossed me a Molson from the ice chest, and I leaned back on the counter. I opened the beer and watched as Hank began to dance along to the song titled "For What It's Worth." He cut down the aisles with long, graceful strides, moving well for a man of his stature. He disappeared behind a row of potato chips and returned with a bottled Coca Cola in his hand. He started to use the bottle as a microphone, belting out the lyrics as he danced, and I couldn't help but sing along when he reached the chorus. Man, did it feel great.

The song ended, and my wristwatch was telling me it was time to continue toward my destination of Elm and Market. I finished the Molson and purchased a pack of Camels.

I noticed the Los Angeles Kings game was playing on a small television behind the counter. "Kings look good this year," Hank said as he noticed me watching the game. I didn't know much about hockey, but I told him I thought so, too. As I was about to exit, I remembered why I was drawn to Peterson's in the first place.

"Hank, you seen Charlie tonight?" I asked.

"Afraid not, buddy. Figured he'd be tossing dice out back, but I guess he must be roaming again," replied Hank through his Coca Cola microphone.

Goddammit, Charlie, I cursed to myself, exiting under the pink glow of the sign that flashed "ETERSON's Liquor."

At nine thirty sharp, a black Mercedes sedan pulled to the corner of Elm and Market. I said good-bye to the night air, which was treating me so kindly, and slid into the passenger's seat.

"Good evening, Mr. Buffalo," said the driver sarcastically. "What can I interest the Coast's most desirable bastard in tonight?"

I turned toward the driver, who was grinning ear to ear. His eyes flickered in the dim interior lighting. He could hardly sit still in his seat. A handsome man by the name of Eli Winston Buffalo, my brother. Eli was two years younger than I, which placed him at about twenty-three-and-a-half years old. We were terrifyingly similar in appearance. He had a slim, muscular figure and strong facial features to greet the world with. His face looked as though it may have been symmetrical at one time but was left slightly rugged by some bar scrap and slightly freckled by the California Sun. Upon introduction, strangers would make the obvious comments, linking our similarity in appearance and prompting the question, "Are you guys brothers?" Over time, if the stranger had grown to become a good friend, he would realize that we were essentially one and the same. It should be noted that no one was allowed to call us the *Buffalo Brothers*. We had decided in our youth that the term *Buffalo Brothers* sounded like the name of a hip folk band in which we wanted no association.

I looked over at Eli, who was attempting to light a cigarette with little progress, repeatedly breaking flimsy gas-station matches in his haste. Eventually he gave up and tossed his entire pack of cigarettes, along with the matchbook, out the car window. He flashed a sinister smile and laughed to himself, running a hand through his dirty-blond hair. It was tangled and messy, much like mine had been years earlier when I still felt the need to wear my rebellion. At the time, my hair was clean and parted to the side. You could see my face better that way.

Eli and I were very similar in nature yet orbiting life at slightly different paces. We were both undergoing changes rapidly ever since our father's passing a year ago, I indulging in the *Bad Dharma*, Eli dancing haplessly in the void. Together we were the heirs of the Buffalo estate and a healthy purse to go along with it.

Our father, Charles David Buffalo, had been a wealthy businessman who had consequently made love to many women. It was assumed that Charles Buffalo had a handful of illegitimate children throughout his life. However, Eli and I had never encountered any of them, and we wanted to keep it that way. Charles Buffalo had made a fortune in the stock market at the ripe age of twenty-five, investing in firearms. He was a self-proclaimed genius with little scholarly background. He had always perceived himself as somewhat of a modern cowboy and dressed to fit the part. His hair was long and silver-blond. He wore trophy crocodile boots and a beat-up leather cowboy hat with a matching pocket vest. He claimed to have killed the crocodile for the boots and a thief for the hat and vest. Charles Buffalo was full of shit. He had spent more time traveling than being a father. He documented his travels in a trilogy of memoirs titled *Charles David Buffalo and the Deep Congo*, *Charles David Buffalo and the Pygmy Worshipers*, and his most prized work, *Charles David Buffalo and the Colonization of a Civilized Holy Land*. He completed the latter just days prior to his assassination in Jerusalem. Eli and I never really cared for Charles David Buffalo because he had never really given us anything to care about.

Our mother, Marie Antoinette Billings, named after the late queen of France, met Charles David Buffalo in the Congo while doing missionary work for the Red Cross. Marie Antoinette was seven years younger than the businessman-turned-explorer-turned author. Charles Buffalo was thirty-two at the time. According to *Charles David Buffalo and the Deep Congo*, Charles Buffalo knew the moment he laid eyes on the young missionary worker that she would eventually become the mother of his children. A self-described man of conquest, he "convincingly stole the heart of Marie Antoinette," and the two wed at his hillside mansion back on the Tired Coast. It was said to be the most amazing ceremony the Coast had ever seen—all of California, for that matter. The state's most esteemed actors and musicians took part in the ceremony, drinking the finest champagne and dancing to live music for two days straight. When Marie Antoinette Billings walked down the aisle, it was said that complete silence fell over the estate except for a single violinist, who played softly for the crowd. The guests were left breathless, mesmerized by the bride's iconic beauty. All that could be heard was the whispering violin, the whipping coastal winds that stormed up the bluffs, and the colliding of the surf below. Charles Buffalo revealed in his last novel, *Charles David Buffalo and the Colonization of a Civilized Holy Land*, that this had been the happiest day of his entire life, and if he could bring a fraction of this happiness to the Middle East, then his life would be a great success.

Marie Antoinette Billings-Buffalo died while giving birth to Eli in the fall of 1987. I was two years old at the time and have little understanding or recollection of how exactly my mother passed, other than the fact that there was a complication during my brother's birth. In fact, all I really know about either of my parents is derived from the three novels my father wrote. Charles Buffalo had considered these memoirs to be "works of brilliant truth." However, most readers saw them as slightly fictional. A year after our mother's passing, Charles David Buffalo took off on a series of adventures, afraid to face his two young children. In the epilogue to *Charles David Buffalo and the Colonization of a Civilized Holy Land*, he mentions his regret for not being a good father. However, he felt as though it was never in his blood to be an admirable figure.

Eli and I were raised by Doris Elena Alsworth, a Pulitzer Prize winner in 2001 for her work titled, *The Raising of Eli and James Buffalo: America's Reveling Youth*. An activist in her college days, Doris had come to the Buffalo estate with the intention of gaining a large donation for a coastal clean-up project involving the relocation of California green sea turtle eggs. She was twenty years old at the time and very attractive. She had long blonde hair and soft green eyes that peered inquisitively out of the same oval spectacles she had worn since grammar school. Doris's most attractive quality was the confident and loving manner in which she carried herself. If Charles Buffalo wasn't so distraught from his wife's passing less than a year earlier, he most likely would have made a pass at Doris. Doris, however, was more interested in the two children who were draped around Charles David Buffalo's size-eleven crocodile boots. Instantly recognizing Doris's attraction to the children, Charles Buffalo hired her on the spot as a live-in caretaker. Three days later, Charles Buffalo was gone and left this note:

Boys,

Doris is your mother now. Be good.

Charles David Buffalo

When Charles Buffalo left, Doris had free rein in all matters regarding the Buffalo estate. She wasted no time in renovating the West Wing of the mansion into a library study. The ceilings were naturally high in the West Wing, and she saw to it that they were stacked full of literature. Eli and I spent a great deal of time in the study, nose-deep in Doris's favorite novels. At a young age, we became familiar with Barrie, Twain, and Vonnegut. My favorite novel was Vonnegut's *The Sirens of Titan*, which Doris used to read to me before I fell asleep. It is probably not the most romantic children's novel, but I always had the best dreams of space and life on the paradise known as Titan. I had often wished that I, too, could live amongst the Titanic Bluebirds, they sounded so wonderful. I liked *The Adventures of Tom Sawyer*, too.

Much to the groundskeeper's dismay, Doris requested that two tons of soil be placed in the center of the study. She then asked the staff to relocate the estate's largest spruce tree into the study. This upset most all of the servants, who began fleeing in droves, claiming Doris had lost her mind. Once the great spruce tree had been set in place, the remaining servants were instructed to build an equally grand tree house for Eli, Doris, and me to read in. Skylights were installed above the large tree, and an irrigation system was put underneath the floorboards. We never wanted to leave the study, and we opted to sleep in the tree house, which was then furnished with two twin beds. Eli and I spent our youth swinging from the tree house balcony, reenacting Barrie's *Peter Pan*. We argued over which one of us got to be Peter Pan, but it was foolish because we were both just two lost boys.

Doris had Eli and me work on stories of our own. After school all three of us would write together in the tree house. Doris dedicated *The Raising of Eli and James Buffalo: America's Reveling Youth* to "her little writing buddies."

When Eli and I outgrew the tree house's twin beds and moved from the study into separate bedrooms in the East Wing, the three of us stopped reading and writing together. That fall, Eli stopped writing entirely, and Doris continued to live in the guesthouse, despite our insistence she move inside the mansion with us. I continued to write on my own in the East Wing. I read

The Perks of Being a Wallflower when I was a teenager, and I thought the main character, Charlie, cried too much. My writing got darker as I got older, and Doris said I was getting better. By the time I turned twenty, I had managed to write two dumb novels, which I loved very much at times. Doris edited them both.

Doris's presence in our lives had been reduced within the last year, as she was working on her much-awaited and long-overdue second novel. In fact, we hadn't seen much of Doris since our father died and I started seeing Doctor Henry P. Whitehouse. We could tell she was hard at work, as the upstairs lamps stayed lit into the early hours of the morning. It was nice to know Doris was still watching over us.

—  —

Eli opened the car door and stepped outside of the black sedan to retrieve the pack of cigarettes he had tossed out earlier.

"Do you have a light?" he said upon returning to the sedan. "I fucking hate these matches, but the style is too damn good." I reached into my pocket and produced a flame while Eli drew breath, filling the car with a puff of smoke.

"So tell me, how's the old man? He got any worldly revelations for you today?" he asked with a crooked grin.

"Nothing too great," I said, feeling the booze and tea move around in my stomach.

"Did he make you paint again?" he asked, and I just shrugged. "That fucking kook..." Eli muttered to himself. I pretended not to hear him as I rolled down the passenger window and invited the cool air back into the car.

"I like painting," I said after a second or so, and when I think about it, strangely, I can't really remember much from my appointment with the Doctor. I hand Eli the purple bottle in my breast pocket.

"So this is where the old man keeps all the answers," he said and shook the bottle up and down. The rattling sound gave me chills as I remembered some of what the Doctor and I talked about.

"He just asked a lot of questions about Doris, man. He always wants to talk about Doris, and every time I tell him, hey, I have not seen her lately, can we talk about something else! But we talk about her nonetheless, and he just smiles and says, 'Good, good.'"

"Hmmm, that *is* strange," replied Eli with a twinge of concern on his face as he poured the pills out on the dash. I didn't mind sharing when I had enough. I was thinking about taking one more myself when Doris's words resonated in my head: "Just think, in a few years you will be the one walking Eli to school." I looked at my little brother and I resisted the urge to take another pill. And I felt terrible but did not say anything when Eli took three pills for himself. It hurt because we were so far beyond schoolyard walks.

When Charles David Buffalo died, Eli and I inherited his life savings and a majority share in Smith & Wesson. Eli was free to do as he wanted with his first share of the inheritance, which was about four and a half million. He had access to his half at all times.

My conditions were different. Due to a proscribed and well-documented mental lapse a few summers prior to my father's death, I was required to seek the guidance of Doctor Henry P. Whitehouse in order to receive my inheritance. My father made it clear in his Last Will and Testament that he believed I was insane. When he died my existing trust was revoked and new conditions were put in place. Charles David Buffalo was determined to protect his legacy.

If I were a better man I would not need *his* money, but like I said, I wasn't strong enough to take that leap. I had no real income of my own at the time; my novels weren't selling very well, and I hadn't written anything new in years. And once I started to see Doctor Henry P. Whitehouse, I realized I liked the way his modern pills made me feel. I was deep inside the *Bad Dharma*, so I agreed to these conditional visits to nurse my heavy fears of contemporary social failure and live off my inheritance. I had been seeing Doctor Whitehouse for about a year, and I could tell this upset Doris, as she became distant. Charles David Buffalo's reason for creating the stipulation in his Last Will and Testament was simple: He felt I was not sane enough to "preserve his legacy." He had his reasons. I had embarrassed him when I broke down a few years before he died. And I had always been a little off. For my tenth birthday, Charles David Buffalo gave me a thousand dollars and a birthday card that read:

James,

Happy twelfth birthday! The Congo is nice. Spend well. Your Father,

Charles David Buffalo

The card was covered with cigar burns as though Charles David Buffalo had used it as an ashtray. I took the thousand dollars and went down to the old pet shop on Farris and Market and I bought thirty birds. The owner didn't have all thirty birds that day, so he gave me thirteen, and I collected the other seventeen over the next few weeks. I didn't care what kind of birds they were. Primarily, he gave me parrots and canaries. Charles David Buffalo had built a bird sanctuary, which had long since been abandoned, near the rear of the estate. I had been keeping the birds there. And once I had collected all thirty birds I invited Eli and Doris out to the backyard for a "special show." I let all thirty of the birds out of the sanctuary. It was the most beautiful thing I have ever seen. Doris hugged me and told me she loved me as the birds flew out over the ocean.

I imagine this upset Charles David Buffalo. I didn't receive a thirteenth birthday card when I turned eleven, or any other card from then on out. Doris thought it was the sweetest thing—the birds, that is.

When I turned twenty-two I just wanted to feel alive. I spent hours in front of the mirror just trying to cry because I thought I should. Something had changed; I wanted my birds back, but they were all gone. I wanted them back so I could let them go again. And I wanted her to be proud of me again.

I wanted to shave my head and cut my beard, but it had all been done before. *Everything had been done before,* I thought—and this thought drove me insane. I reread *The Perks of Being a Wallflower*, and I thought that the main character, Charlie, was a fucking saint. I couldn't find a single tear or anything genuine at all. I no longer felt human, and I wasn't exactly sure what was standing in front of my bathroom mirror. I walked calmly out of the bathroom and into the study. I climbed the tree house. And in a fit of sadness, I threw myself over the railing and broke my right arm. I looked at my crooked arm and I still felt nothing. So, I went to the supermarket to buy some oranges, and when I got to the produce aisle I started to feel the sharpest pain in my arm. Sure I could drink it off, I headed toward aisle ten, where they kept the booze. They found me face down in between aisles six and seven. I have been trying to chill out ever since. My father died two years after this incident.

Eli doesn't think I am crazy, though he is probably not the most reliable source when it comes to things like this. Nor was his opinion the one that mattered. Charles David Buffalo thought I was crazy, and I was finding out that it's very hard to change a dead man's mind. I was stuck inside of my old man's Will and Testament, until I found something better.

So, I leaned comfortably back in the passenger's seat. And I watched as Eli slid the key into the ignition. I couldn't help but smile as the interior lights dimmed, I felt the smooth rumbling of the engine beneath me, music started from the car's stereo, and with a jerk, the black sedan took off gently into the night. Eli spent the next five minutes talking quickly, filling me in on the girls he had picked up earlier in the day. I smiled and nodded along. He swore I was going to die for this sweet brunette named Sara he had found at the farmers' market. I thought this girl might have some potential because I usually fell for girls at the farmers' market. Eli was dead set on making it with her blonde friend and adjusted his tangled hair in the rearview mirror. The car swerved as he dodged a parked car, and I started to laugh. Eli was a terrible driver, and I wasn't much better myself, so I kept my mouth shut. When we were together everything was fine. The streetlights were beginning to blur together in a chemical swirl. I slowly turned the volume knob on the radio and let the music run through me. Everything was honey as the plucking of an unorthodox acoustic guitar guided us through the darkness.

CHAPTER
— 3 —

After leaving the city, Eli and I decided to meet up with the girls he had met at the farmers' market the previous afternoon. They wanted to have drinks at The Gull, a small oceanfront bar. My spirits were high and I was up for anything, so when we proceeded into the bar with little trouble, I couldn't help but smile at the crowd of men and women. The scene was rather messy, but pleasant nonetheless. Inside, The Gull smelled of smoke, spilt beer, and a clashing of perfumes, which when combined created the standard aroma associated with any American bar.

The Gull had two levels. The lower level, where we stood, was reserved for the eager type. The type that had to look "right" before coming undone, the type that bled hair gel, the type that drank for the courage to seem "normal." The upper level was reserved for the tired type, the type with tired eyes. The tired type that desperately needed the ocean breeze to chase away the harshest of spirits, usually whiskey.

Upstairs Eli introduced me to his girl, Lucia Lethridge. She was alone, lounging in a candlelit booth, smoking a half-gone cigarette. I had to admit she was really gorgeous, a skinny yet healthy girl with tight hips that could sway naturally to any rhythm. She wore ruby-red lipstick that would make a lesser woman seem trashy and drank hard to prove she had troubles to match her beauty. We ordered drinks as the surf sounded off through the darkness and Lucia's fair skin glistened underneath the pallid moon. Eli carried the conversation for most of the evening. Lucia watched with admiration as Eli spoke. I hoped she liked me the same, though it was irrelevant considering she was already Eli's girl. As the drinks began to disappear, it became apparent that Lucia's brunette friend, Sara, was not going to show. It was fine, though; really it was. I never had much game in bars anyway.

When Eli took a break from talking, to smoke one of his last cigarettes, Lucia spoke of how she had traveled all the way from San Luis Obispo hitchhiking on the back of agricultural trucks. Sometimes wooing potential drivers by walking seductively down the highway, hips swaying to the breeze, arm and thumb extended in the traditional hitchhiker's form. I was previously under the assumption that hitchhiking in America was dead. However, I supposed a good-looking woman was always a welcomed passenger. Eli and I both agreed that she was far too pretty to do such a thing, and we offered to pay for any future travel accommodations, but Lucia just laughed and said, "Oh please, I've got enough spirit for the both of you... and you're right, boys, I am *too pretty.*" She finished with a wink, wrinkling her tiny nose in the cutest way possible.

"Charming," said Eli, doing his best to mockingly wrinkle his nose in the same way Lucia had. I watched as Lucia's proud cheeks turned an uncomfortable pink. Eli could be mean, and girls liked him for this. I felt terrible, though, absolutely terrible; I was the only one allowed to be vulnerable. I needed to act.

"Oh, I believe her," I said grabbing our waiter's arm as he passed our table. "Excuse me," I said to the man. "It's getting late and we've all had too much to drink. My brother and I have business up in Orange County tomorrow morning, and, you see, our good friend here," I motioned toward Lucia, "well, she has to be in Mexico City by sunrise to meet a high-end diplomat. I know it's a bad time down south, with the Cartel's madness, but I need you to ask the staff if they would be willing to give her a ride. Tonight."

"I'll ask," said the man half amused, half annoyed.

"See," I said, nodding like Lloyd Christmas, "she's a total babe!" And we all laughed. I felt a lot better now that I had made a fool of myself. "Excuse me," I said. "I have to use the restroom." I got up from the table and left Eli and Lucia behind. The only restroom was downstairs, so I stopped by the bar on my way. I ordered a shot from the bartender and dropped my elbows down to relax. A television was playing highlights from the Lakers game. The Lakers had just lost to the Grizzlies, and Kobe Bryant appeared as though he wanted to murder the entire team.

"That was cute," I heard a voice say. I turned around and saw the waiter I had stopped standing behind me. "Oh," I replied looking back at the television. "The whole Mexico City thing," he said. "I hope it works; she is very attractive."

The bartender came back with my shot; I took it and motioned for him to pour another. "We are about to close," the waiter spoke again. "Your brother said you would pay the tab." I noticed the young man had the bill in his hands. "That's fine," I said. "Put it on the bar."

The tab ran me dry. I signed the bill just as the bartender started to pour me a second shot. I told him to stop. I turned around and sheepishly handed the bill to the waiter. The tab was about a hundred dollars. I had left him only four dollars and thirty-seven cents as a tip. The man opened the fold and looked at me like Kobe had looked at his teammates after the loss.

"Too bad," he said shaking his head. "She is a pretty girl, but Mexico City... " Without thinking I shook some pills loose from the purple bottle I had stowed in my jacket pocket. I pulled the waiter in close to me as I stood up to leave. "Don't forget sunscreen," I whispered handing him some pills.

"I never do," he replied with a crooked smile. "I never do."

Satisfied, I stumbled down the short flight of stairs to the lower level, where the bass from the oversized speakers proceeded to kill my eardrums. I kicked open the swinging restroom doors like a Western hero entering a low-life saloon. I then took the longest piss of my life, I swear.

When I was done, I went outside to smoke a cigarette and look at the stars. I was standing on the sidewalk with my head turned upward, in a heavenly awe, feeling universally small, when Eli and Lucia joined me.

"James, you bastard!" shouted Eli, wrapping an arm around my shoulder. "I thought you were nuts, but they fucking bought it, man, they fucking bought it."

"Huh," I replied pulling away from the flickering sky.

"Huh?" Eli laughed like a maniac. "Huh is right! You're a fucking riot, James. Four dudes on the staff offered to give Lucia a ride to Mexico-fucking-city, tonight! They were practically tripping over her." I smiled as Lucia blushed in a good way.

"I knew they would," I said.

"And guess what, James," Eli started again. "We're hitching home tonight; I already came up with the plan!"

Eli's plan was simple. The three of us would walk out toward Highway 101, where Lucia would flag down a vehicle. Eli and I were to hide behind the guardrail. Lucia was going to stop something with a flatbed so that Eli and I could stow away undetected as she flirted with the driver. "It's fish in a barrel, man," Eli said as he finished diagramming the plan on a crumpled bar napkin.

In what seemed like a matter of seconds, we were up on Highway 101, hopping the rusted guardrail. The evening's drinking had caused my mind to loosen and fade from attention. I snapped back to life just as Lucia rubbed our heads and said, "Three's a crowd, boys." And she was right. Eli and I were in bad shape, full of bloodshot eyes and queer smiles. No one in his or her right mind would willingly take us on as passengers. We were sure to either throw up in their cab or steal their money, perhaps both.

Eli's plan sprung into full effect a few mindless minutes later as a faded blue pickup pulled to a halt some twenty yards ahead. I could barely make out the dented license plate, which read 457XR4W. I made a drunken effort to memorize it in case something went wrong. A light came on in the cab of the pickup, and Lucia's heels excitedly clicked to life as she stood in front of us.

"This is it, this is..." Eli said clutching my right bicep. Lucia hiked up her skirt a bit and pushed her cleavage together.

"Get ready to run, boys," she whispered. She then turned away from us on a quick heel, cocked her head upward, and blew a kiss to the moon.

"I love her," Eli said to me as we watched Lucia approach the cab, our feet pressed flat in anticipation. "I absolutely love her, James."

I didn't say anything. Instead, I focused intently on the truck. Lucia was sliding into the passenger's seat at the moment. As she did so, she dropped her clutch. This was our signal. Lucia bent over like a sexual firework, and the driver's eyes followed as she pretended to feel around for her clutch. Together, Eli and I hopped the guardrail and ran like two mad lunatics into the night.

CHAPTER
— 4 —

I awoke to the cooing of mourning doves as the thinnest ray of sunshine crept through the blinds, softly kissing my face. The fleeting light exposed every particle of dust on its way to me like a telescope revealing planets in July. I took turns opening and closing each of my eyes, watching childishly as the light appeared to dance back and forth across the room. I pulled straight and put my feet on the cold Spanish tile and focused on the alarm clock, which flashed 8:14 A.M. I almost felt guilty for not being hung over, though it was quite possible I was still sauced. I reached for the nightstand and administered my daily prescriptions, accumulating enough saliva in my mouth to swallow my recommended dosage of MRX2857: three pills.

I could hear laughter from the kitchen below, accompanied by racing footsteps.

I heard the crash of what sounded like a large flowerpot shattering downstairs, which was followed by a great burst of laughter. Eli, Lucia, and I had successfully hitchhiked home from the bar the previous night. I looked down and saw my jeans dirtied and crumpled on the floor. They were stained with manure all across the backside; the bed of the blue pickup had been full of it. I could faintly make out Lucia's voice downstairs.

"You stop right now, Eli Winston Buffalo!" she half yelled. "You're going to wake up James!"

Hearing Lucia say my name filled my body with a rush of excitement, and I pulled the blinds up, exposing my bare chest to the Sun. I heard another crash, followed again by roaring laughter. I threw on an old shirt, determined to take part in the early-morning commotion.

I flung myself down the spiral staircase with great ease, in such a manner that one could only achieve on significantly pleasant days. I rounded the lower East Hall, striding swiftly into the kitchen. Immediately I had to duck as an unknown object whizzed past my left ear and collided with the wall.

"Good morning, James!" screamed Eli, who was holding a large stack of ceramic plates in his hands. He chuckled. "What-a-day, what-a-day!"

It was obvious he had spent the night with Lucia, and as any man should be after spending the night with such a woman, he was in extremely good spirits. I ducked again as another plate came whizzing my way. I managed to dodge it just before it crashed in the hallway behind me.

"That's it!" I screamed playfully, and I chased Eli around the room until we lost our breath. I captured my brother behind the kitchen island, wrestled him to the ground, and placed one foot atop his chest. Raising my right arm in an official manner, I declared myself to be the one rightful owner of the Buffalo estate. I then ordered that Lucia behead this treacherous plate-breaker with a nearby wooden rolling pin. She proceeded with the fake execution, and we joined Eli on the floor, rolling in laughter.

"You know, it's too bad Sara couldn't come last night, James," said Lucia. I told her that it was fine, but she promptly replied, "I just really think she would like you, that's all, you silly boy."

Eli then injected his two cents into the matter by stating that if she couldn't show last night, she couldn't be trusted for anything in the future, and this could prove to be problematic.

I laughed and once more assured Lucia that there were no hard feelings and my brother was an idiot. I told her that I looked forward to meeting Sara at a later date. "Plus," I said, "I doubt Sara would have wanted to ride in the back of the truck with us. I still smell like cow shit."

"You'd be surprised, James," Lucia said with her patented wink. "Some girls don't mind getting dirty."

— ✿ —

On days when the Sun hangs high and the blues of ocean and the sky blur together, it is hard to remember why anyone has ever felt a trickle of sadness. Lucia wanted to go for a swim in the estate's swimming pool. However, Eli and I convinced her that the beach would be a much more desirable location. Without a moment's hesitation, all three of us headed up the spiral staircase in search of the proper attire. Eli tried convincing Lucia to go down to the shore in her undergarments, though much to our disappointment, she refused. Instead she emerged wearing a pair of Eli's short polka-dot swim trunks. I had always thought the old shorts looked good on my brother, but I began to see they fit Lucia in a much more flattering way. Her top half was covered in one of Eli's old tank tops, which she had tucked confidently into the shorts.

"I know, I know. I look horrendous, but it's all you have, so please don't judge me, boys," Lucia said, though no one believed her insincere tone. She knew she could look beautiful in anything, and she did.

Without a second to waste, we exited through the study, which spat us out on the west lawn where Marie Antoinette Billings and Charles David Buffalo had wed many years before. The grass was taller, having grown wild for months following the departure of the estate's last groundskeeper in September. Tall daisies sprouted through the sea of green. I picked the best one and gave it to Lucia. It was hard to believe such a beautiful day could exist in what had been such a cold December. The birds sang loudly, and there was no sound of the surf crashing below, which meant the beach would be exposed. The three of us tore through the high grass toward the old wooden staircase that would guide us down the bluffs. Pausing halfway in a patch of wildflowers, I looked back toward the study and thought I could see Doris reading in the tree house. The study's large bay windows were cracked open, and the wind crept through, silently pushing her blonde hair as she read. When I turned back for another glance, the tree house was empty, and the tire swing swayed solemnly in the breeze; for a brief second I felt very old.

At the edge of the bluffs I could make out several white sails moving across the horizon. When I was younger, I would always ask Doris if the *white things* were sharks, and she always replied, "Yes, the meanest, James!" I still sometimes imagine the white sails are sharks.

As we reached the bottom of the wooden stairs, Eli and I jumped the remaining three and a half feet to the beach below. I watched as Lucia placed her small hands in Eli's and made the jump for herself. When she landed, her breasts pressed against Eli's chest, and he wrapped his arms around her narrow shoulders.

Barefoot in the soft, sinking sand, I felt the scales of jealousy sliding into my heart, and I burrowed my toes deep into the cool sand. For a second, I thought I saw Lucia glance my way. I wanted to kiss her right there on the beach in front of Eli. And I felt a little depressed even beneath the blue sky.

"Look, sharks! Sharks, James!" blurted Eli, who pretended to fly across the shore with his arms in a winged position.

"The meanest!" I replied.

The west side of the Buffalo estate faced the great Pacific Ocean and had access to a remote beach. The only way to reach the beach was either to sail into the cove itself or walk down the Buffalos' private staircase. Considering it was public knowledge that the Buffalos owned practically half of Smith & Wesson, most people thought better of trespassing. The beach was only a half-mile long and was protected by protruding bluffs on the north and south ends, creating a horseshoe-shaped inlet. I usually spent a good deal of the summer months drinking and meditating with my back pressed against the California jade plants that grew along the bottom of the bluffs.

The guest residence stood atop the calmer south end, facing the old lighthouse, which resided on the more rugged northern cliff. The lighthouse in its modesty usually looked like a lone tree on a sad mountain. However, that day when I looked up at the lighthouse, it didn't seem so solemn. In fact it seemed to gesture some kind of hello, a proud greeter of the ocean as it came to find land.

"Ahoy!" I said, thinking aloud.

"Huh?" questioned Eli, who had circled back toward the stairs. He was struggling to light a cigarette, breaking match after match.

"Nothing," I said, even though I thought I had found *something* in that old lighthouse. And looking away from the rigid northern peak, I focused on Lucia, who was already barefoot and had stripped off Eli's baggy tank top, bending her skinny frame to collect seashells in nothing but a bra and those polka-dot shorts. I tossed Eli the lighter, turning toward the horizon. He caught the Bic in motion and cut through the open beach, leaving his footprints in the soft sand like a deer at first snowfall.

I felt bad for wanting Lucia. *It's clutter, it's all clutter*, I thought, but damn she was so cool. I reached into my back pocket, grabbed a cigarette, and pretended to light it off the burning Sun. *To hell with the Dharma*, I thought, wishing I had my pills. I wanted to see all those great Chinese poets look at Lucia here on the beach without a trickle of lust as the froth from the shallow surf crept up her skinny legs and hung around her kneecaps.

"Hey! Whaddaya say we show Lucia the caves!" Eli broke my bad thoughts from about one hundred yards distance, as he was once again pretending to fly along the water's edge.

"The caves?" questioned Lucia, who turned her gaze toward me.

"Yes, you can see the entrance there," I said and pointed toward the base of the northern cliff.

Lucia stepped close to me and I began to feel uncomfortable. I could feel her warm breath on my neck, like the incoming tide. My eyes were fixated on Eli, who appeared to be having some sort of engine trouble as he swerved sporadically into the shallows. I could tell what was going to happen next. I turned toward Lucia to tell her "no," but it was too late as she planted a kiss on my open lips and took off toward the caves in a sprint.

The old caves were a favorite of mine. Eli and I used to smoke cigarettes in them when we were teenagers. At night we would light lanterns and cross the beach nervously, on the lookout for any signs of Doris. As I approached the northern base, Eli and Lucia were already ascending the sharp rocks, passing the first two lower caves and approaching the upper cave, where Eli and I had gotten high so many years ago. I could no longer smoke pot without unraveling like an old Christmas sweater.

I didn't really miss it that much—smoking pot, that is—and when Lucia lit a joint I had no trouble in declining. Instead I turned my head upward toward the cave ceiling and sat on my hands, as if to cement the fact that I didn't want to partake in the festivities. I suppose I should have felt some sense of pride in that, though I really felt nothing except a little embarrassment. The flickering of the lighter briefly illuminated the surrounding walls, exposing a vast array of teenage cave art. In minutes, the small cave was filled with smoke, and things began to get hazy, so I poked my head outside the opening to chase some fresh air. From outside looking in, the cave looked like an old adobe chimney pot, producing the thinnest trail of smoke as though a great fire had just died inside its belly. A gentle breeze pushed the purple lavender surrounding the cave, releasing a pleasant aroma to accompany that of the cannabis.

Returning to the cave, I ran my hands across an elephant I had carved when I was thirteen. I had to brush back a few layers of dust before it was returned to its original form.

"I love it!" exclaimed Lucia as she exhaled pot smoke into the cramped cave, which I remembered as being much larger when I was younger.

"Uh, yeah, it smells dank," I replied clumsily.

Lucia giggled.

"She is talking about the elephant, dumbass," Eli said before pulling gently from the joint, exhaling smoke through his nose, his eyes tiny and beet red. "Although, you're right, it is *dank*."

I wanted to punch Eli in his face (which looked a lot like mine) as he smiled, slyly leaning against the back wall. His tongue pushed outward like a snake's, and he licked the side of the joint to slow the burning. He turned to pass the joint to Lucia, and I contemplated catching him behind the head. Instead I thought of Lucia's soft lips pressing against mine.

"Yes and yes," stated Lucia, who was too high to notice the tension. "Love the elephant, James, and . . . ," she inhaled deeply, "...the weed is good, too, Eli." She slid her fingers across the elephant's tusk and let go of the smoke in her lungs. "Say, what's coming out of its mouth?" she asked.

"It's throwing up," I replied, red hot with embarrassment.

"Why, is it sick?" Lucia exclaimed. She turned from the wall to face Eli, who was standing upright in a bit of laughter—not quite ready to let it go.

"No," spoke Eli, stretching his arms up to the roof of the cave. "James thinks he is a shaman, so you will notice all the animals he has carved are vomiting."

Lucia lit her lighter once more and held its flame long enough to fully examine the crude art that covered the walls. Eli was right. Almost all the animals I had created were throwing up.

I watched as Lucia focused on a sickly dinosaur. "So, is it true? Are you a shaman?" Lucia questioned softly.

"Yeah, most definitely," I replied, staring out the cave's entrance toward the incoming surf, knowing very well that I was not.

"So, is that what shamans do? Draw animals throwing up?" she asked attempting to draw smoke from the fading roach.

"Amongst other things," I said, fighting tears.

"Like what!" she cried.

I coughed. "Shamans can do lots of things."

"Like...?"

"For starters, we can fly in our dreams and talk to animals as well." I watched curiously as Lucia's glassy eyes lit up. I felt my sails lift on the winds of confidence, once again thinking of how she had kissed me. "We're actually of great importance. You see, I have visions where I see... uh... uh..." I started to think that I might be a little high as well, even though I didn't smoke. "I... uh... I mean shamans..."

Lucia smiled. "Come on, James, spit it out. What do you see?"

"We can see the future, but it's not always clear. Most shamans see the future through hallucinations, myself included. These visions can be both frightening and strange. It is a sporadic process that produces very important information with little credibility or valor. Much like the CIA," I said, and she laughed. "I enjoy the flying dreams very much, though. Have you ever had a flying dream?"

"No, but I am flying right now!" Lucia shouted, and we started to laugh. Eli, too, even though I could tell he didn't want to.

"I am sure you are," I said, looking back out over the glassy ocean.

"Well, I'm going to call you Peter from now on!" she shrieked and giggled with a child's innocence. "Look, Eli, it's Peter Pan!"

Eli laughed again, though I could tell this—the attention I was receiving—was upsetting him, as he began to pace back and forth in the cave's limited space. Once again we were two young children in the tree house at arms over who was fit to be Peter Pan.

"Well, if I am Peter, then you must be my Wendy," I said to Lucia and watched as Eli's cheeks turned bright red when I held out my empty hand, pretending to reveal a thimble. "Would you like a kiss?"

"Why, that's not a real kiss, Peter!" Lucia said quietly, staring right through me. She then dramatically flopped herself down against the cave wall, and we all laughed till my stomach hurt and I felt real sour. Lucia had given me a *real kiss* on the beach. I wish it had been a thimble.

I needed to stay in the present think, and as the sea air crept through the cave on a whisper, it brought in the easy smell of lavender and managed to soothe my wandering soul for the time being.

Lavender was Doris's favorite, and when it was in bloom she would oftentimes hang it throughout the house. I could sense Doris's presence in the cave, and I could tell I was not alone in the feeling.

Eli smiled as the red left his cheeks. "Well, I guess that makes me Captain Hook." He glanced at me calmly with love in his eyes, a love great and androgynous; he was my brother.

"And I'm afraid you're coming with me, Wendy!" he shouted, forming his hand in the shape of a hook and pretending to lunge after Lucia.

Lucia smiled, her hands on her soft cheeks. "Oooohh Captain, you're so sexy. Let me wear your hat, will you not?"

"Never!" He lunged again.

"I'll steal you that old hat, Wendy!" I said as I dove forward and pretended to fall, catching myself on the dirt wall.

Eli waved his hands about victoriously. "Why, what's a captain without his hat!" "Plus..." Eli leaned toward Lucia and whispered, "what would Peter..." he nodded in my direction, "...say if he knew I was bald?"

CHAPTER
— 5 —

From my window, high and safe in the East Wing, I could make out the guests arriving in small groups. They were trickling in underneath the estate's arched entryway, which was overrun with ivy.

I lifted the needle of the old family record player and I pulled lightly from my cigarette. I placed the needle back down softly and listened as it went *scratch, scratch*. The cold wind blew through the night, and the arriving guests pulled their collars up high and tight. The same wind crept through my window and caused the curtains to rise like dancing ghosts.

I looked out over the estate as Neutral Milk Hotel's live recording of "Little Birds" began to play. The live record was a rarity I had found buried in the back of a thrift shop on Haight Ashbury. Had to love hipsters and their willingness to buy, sell, and trade vintage gems. The song was a sad song. Jeff Mangum even said so in the beginning. It was about a boy who lives in a sad world and one day invents in his mind a thousand little birds. I imagine the birds to be tiny bluebirds. The birds magically fill the boy's room, pouring in from the water faucet and into his body through his open mouth. The boy is very happy about this. However, when he tells others what has happened, they get upset and try to destroy the beauty the boy has found. I imagine the boy's parents make him see a doctor or something, Jeff Mangum doesn't really say. The song was sad, but the melody was sweet as roses. I couldn't help but hum along.

I should have been embarrassed about the condition of the yard. From my window I could see what a mess it had become. Truthfully, I could care less. I imagined old friends of Charles David Buffalo speaking amongst each other sourly. Whispering how clean and beautiful the lawn had been many years ago when Charles David Buffalo and Marie Antoinette Billings had wed. "Of course," they would say, "that was before James went insane."

I could make out a tall blonde with a feathered peacock mask making her way toward the entrance, accompanied by a short, chubby man with a thin, black comb-over. The pair was undoubtedly Mr. and Mrs. Humphrey. Cynthia Humphrey stopped to adjust her cleavage in the reflection produced between the moon and the window of our black sedan, which was parked crookedly in the driveway.

Taking the time to apply one last coat of thick, blood-red lipstick, Mrs. Humphrey called for her husband to quit "pussyfooting around the roses." Her short bowling ball of a husband, Donald M. Humphrey, was hobbling not far behind. He was admittedly at a disadvantage due to the fact his right leg had been injured in an automobile accident some years before. As a result he walked with a heavy limp and had to use a wooden cane for balance.

Donald Humphrey owned Humphrey Farms, a major West Coast distributor of sausage and hamburger meat. A very wealthy man who enjoyed his product a little too much. He was a fair man, though, and I respected him for this. He always treated his employees with the utmost respect and dignity, earning him "best business" honors in the *Herald West's* "Top Employers to Work For" column. Most men would probably deem his wife, Cynthia Humphrey, to be attractive. She was a prototypical "blonde bombshell," so to speak. Personally, I found her a rather fake broad, and I often pitied Donald Humphrey because of this.

Another group of guests arrived at that moment, emerging from a stretch limousine. The group paused beneath the ivy-covered entrance to fasten masks to their faces. Because they were hidden in the shadow of the archway, I could not recognize any of these guests. I heard an anonymous face exclaim underneath the ivy, "I never liked these goddamn charity banquets."

It was the ninth annual charity ball for the Chrysanthemum Foundation, a donation-based charity Doris had created nearly a decade earlier. The Chrysanthemum Foundation provided flowers to terminally ill patients in hospitals nationwide. Doris's belief was that the presence of life prolongs life itself. She would always get so upset thinking about the hypothetical poor old man who had no one to buy him flowers, the man's last memory on Earth being the cheap hospital art hanging crookedly in his room, maybe a crappy mass-produced painting of a sailboat, or something like that. The Chrysanthemum Foundation's goal was to make sure these patients had fresh flowers in their rooms. I am not a religious man; however, it would be nice to go out smelling California roses, or perhaps the ocean. To me that would be *heavenly*.

A few years after the Chrysanthemum Foundation's establishment in 2001, western philanthropists ranging from computer moguls to movie stars started sending in donations. Doris had appeared on CNN, and she even gained Oprah's attention shortly thereafter. The Chrysanthemum Foundation quickly expanded from a few western hospitals to hospitals across the nation.

The Chrysanthemum Foundation used to be run solely by Doris. However, her reclusion of late had caused Eli and me to take a hand in seeing to it that everything ran smoothly. Doris didn't even bother showing up to the previous year's charity ball, something that still bothered the both of us.

I doubted Doris would make an appearance that evening, and with a sigh, I emptied the last remaining contents of my silver flask into a drinking glass filled with ice. I began to rummage through the depths of my closet. Eventually I found what I was looking for, a small fox mask and accompanying tail. The mask was skinny and covered just my nose and the rings around my eyes. I placed the glass of whiskey on top of my dresser and tied the mask tight while gazing into the standing bedroom mirror. I clipped the bushy tail to my back belt loop and reached into the dresser, pulling out an unmarked bottle of whiskey. I refilled the flask and placed it in my back left pocket.

I tilted my drinking glass until I felt the cold cubes press against my lips. Exiting the room, I tried to place the empty glass on top of a bookshelf near the door. I missed by a few inches and the glass hit the tile floor with a cymbal-like crash.

In the hallway, the lights were dimmed and I started toward the stairs. I could hear music and shouting from the party below. Halfway down the hall I paused in front of a wooden mannequin that was dressed in a full suit of armor. The armor was a gift from one of Charles David Buffalo's English friends, Geraldo F. Victoria—a drinking buddy of the royal infantry. The two had met in the Congo. Victoria had been stationed there to extract ivory on a royal mission directed by the Queen of England. Charles David Buffalo was commissioned to the Congo by his own sick will. Victoria was a bloodthirsty drunk, whereas Charles David Buffalo was simply full of shit; naturally they were great companions. I stared directly into the expressionless armor face with disgust. I imagined it coming to life. The East Hall began to tremble, and then everything went still. The ears on my red-fox mask went curiously erect as I froze.

In a flash of red, Victoria's eyes appeared behind the mannequin's armored helmet, burning like two hell-coals. The armor creaked as Victoria's spirit forced the metal hands toward my neck. He loosened his jaw with a single circular motion, and I swear I could hear him whisper through the decades. *Yes, the Queen will like you. What a pretty coat you have. Stay still now.*

I felt the cold metal gloves constrict around my throat like two jungle snakes. My boots lifted from the ground as Victoria's ghost hoisted me upward. Suspended in mid-air, my eyes locked with his—I knew then I had met the Devil. And I could tell he was angry with me because a hellish smoke began to billow out of the armored helmet, filling the East Hall with a putrid smell of rum and dust.

The metal grew tighter around my neck as my bones quivered and then went limp. My heartbeat accelerated, and panic began to set into my oxygen-starved limbs. I desperately ran my hands across the crested armor searching for anything I could hold onto. I managed to reach the handle of Victoria's sword. It was fashioned securely in a scabbard along his waistline. I wrapped my dumb hands around the sword's ivory handle and pulled with every amount of fleeting strength I could muster. It was no use. I couldn't loosen the sword from its scabbard.

Yes, a nice red coat on you, I heard Victoria whisper as my efforts fell flat. My blood began to thin, and I felt my face burn red with suffocation and anger. I thought of how many native hands Victoria had probably chopped off in the Congo in his pursuit of ivory and blood victory.

"You're the redcoat!" I shouted, planting one of my leather boots solidly into the center of the crested armor.

In a rush, the metal and wood crashed to the ground!

I gasped for air as I dropped to my back. Smoke flew across the hall, and I struggled to meet Victoria's ghost, which was wailing loudly. I closed my eyes and pleaded for his cries to stop. Eventually, a quiet peace filled the East Hall. I opened my eyes and found the wooden mannequin and shiny armor vacant, and dismembered, like an old motel. The sword had come loose, and I took it from the lifeless murderer, just like Victoria had taken his trophies in the Congo.

I could hear the dull roar of laughter and music below. Beaming from ear to ear, I slid the sword through my belt loop, and stumbling down the East Wing's spiral staircase, I paused to light a cigarette. I inhaled deeply and slid the pack neatly into my vest pocket. Still breathing hard, I adjusted my bowtie and fastened a smile on as well. After all, I was a gentleman.

The party was truly magnificent. The theme was the same as it was every year, a masked ball. I loved it. There was something truly refreshing about the idea of losing your identity behind a mask, even if just for an evening. That night, at the Buffalo estate, there were actors, writers, politicians, and businessmen. All of the guests were wealthy, and some were there for the humanitarian cause, though most were there to complete a social agenda. The people attending the event for social reasons were most likely accustomed to wearing all sorts of masks during their everyday lives; the party was probably less thrilling for those kinds of people.

Lucia had decorated the interior of the estate so that it held some sort of safari theme. The decor went along with my Congo fantasies and dancing with English armor. Lucia had moved several of Charles David Buffalo's Congo trophies from his office into the living room. I stared at the head of a male lion mounted above the glowing fireplace, and it gave me the creeps. The fire began to dwindle, and a man in an Indian headdress and face paint walked across the room. He started to prod the logs with a fire iron, causing smoke to fill the crowded living room. The man scratched his head clearly dumbfounded. Then, suddenly realizing the draft was closed, the chief extended a thin but muscular arm, and with a jerk he pulled the draft open. Turning on a bare heel, the mysterious Indian disappeared into the crowd of sixty or so masked individuals, who were drinking and socializing over hors d'oeuvres. The man, of course, was Eli. He had worn the same costume for the last nine years.

There were flowers and lots of them, almost every color imaginable. It felt like I was dancing through a seventies dream as I made my way down the stairs, or perhaps maybe an old hippy film—things were fuzzy enough.

I could smell the natural scent of life oozing from the flowers and the burning of the wood from the fireplace. All of these nice things floated through the air and, of course, were met with the scent of perfumes, cologne, and booze. The song was sad, but the melody was sweet as roses.

CHAPTER
— 6 —

I tried to find my brother after he disappeared into the crowd, but there were too many people. I stuck with a group of three broads who were drinking red wine and smoking cigarettes near the back of the party next to the piano, where a man in a white tuxedo sat playing rather well. I was focused on only one person, though—a skinny girl with thin dark hair and olive skin who was holding a deck of cards. She was wearing a silver-glittered mask and a long, black silk dress with a jaguar tail.

"Pick a card," she said, and I did— ace of clubs.

The three girls giggled. A larger girl in a pink neon-feathered mask, a white dress, and matching white gloves extended her hand. She gave me an envelope addressed to the Chrysanthemum Foundation, a check donation.

The girl I was interested in extended her hand to me as I pocketed the envelope. She had a set of three pills in her palms. They were all different colors— blue, salmon pink, and black.

"Aces are black," she said.

"I really shouldn't," I said.

In the game room, things got hazy and warm as semi-anonymous people continued to hand me checks addressed to the foundation. A large man with a curled mustache, wearing a *Phantom of the Opera* mask, was doing lines of cocaine off a silver serving tray on the pool table. So much, in fact, the hair above his upper lip looked as though he had just eaten a powdered doughnut. He smiled and looked right at me.

"I really shouldn't," I said.

For a while, I just sat in the lounging chair across the room. I clapped my hands and sang along freestyle with a crowd of three or four men huddled around a man in an all-burgundy suit. He was strumming an acoustic guitar. The game-room chandelier swayed as my heart began to beat faster and faster.

There was much love back in the main ballroom, where the light was supplied by a few strategically placed lanterns. The piano man was still wailing away when I entered the room. There was movement all around as many elegantly dressed men and women danced close together, sharing laughs and marveling over the estate's grandeur despite its aesthetic neglect. The ballroom walls were still in good condition, except for one auspicious hole in the left wall leading into the living room. A hole Eli had created when he fired one of Charles David Buffalo's rifles a few years back. He had fallen asleep while lounging in a reclining chair. We had been drinking at the bars all night long, and as he nodded off he accidentally pulled the trigger. It was purely accidental and not done out of anger or anything like that. If anything, it was mostly comical. Now it served as a porthole between the ballroom and the living room.

The envelopes kept coming throughout the night as I shook hands with people I had never met (and would most likely never remember) and wrapped my arms around those I knew well. All in all, it was a grand success.

Eventually, I found Eli wrapped up in conversation with a tall, hunkering man at the wooden bar in the back of the ballroom. The large man was drinking whiskey from one of our crystal glasses, so I figured he must be important. Eli was holding the bottle in his left hand, filling the man's glass, his right arm draped over a small blonde in a leopard-print mask and low-cut dress. The little leopard winked at me when I approached the bar and rested my elbows on the old wooden ledge. I pulled a stool out and took a seat next to the man Eli was talking to. I realized by the wink that the little leopard was Lucia and, man, did she ever look good.

I didn't look twice at Lucia, though; my head was still focused on the skinny girl with thin dark hair and olive skin. The one who was holding the deck of cards in which I drew an ace and she giggled. She had given me a black pill. I think it was some sort of prescription pain-killer. It must have been because I was feeling pretty good at the moment except for my stomach. Yeah, my stomach was aching. I could manage, though. Everything appeared to be well.

With a smile I ran a finger along Victoria's blade, which was still tucked between the loop of my belt and the outside of my trousers. I turned away from the bar and looked out toward the crowd of people. I wanted to catch a glimpse of the vixen in the silver mask. I had no such luck. The crowd was too large. Guests filled the ballroom to capacity. People were shouting cheers down from the second-floor hallway, drunkenly spilling drinks on the crowd below.

I felt a hand rubbing the hair on the back of my head, and I turned back toward the bar. Eli was grinning at me behind the bar, his headdress slightly askew and his war paint smudged.

"James, I would like to introduce you to, well, *James*, James De Valle, that is!" Eli said as he motioned to the man standing next to me at the bar. The large man, who was wearing a sleek black tuxedo and a space-themed mask, turned and looked in my direction.

I knew who James De Valle was—an esteemed actor known for his extreme character roles and stunning good looks. His most recent film bent the knees of every starlet in Hollywood, a film titled *The Crooked Man's Broken Window*, an experimental crime drama in which he played the handsome, sick villain who robbed banks and broke hearts. His character was flawed, prone to unusual twitches and quirks. He played the character so well, though, that by the end, you were completely in love with him. And when he was eventually shot dead while looking out his third-story window while taking a sip of hot tea, you wanted to cry, and you probably did.

James De Valle's mask was my favorite, completely black in the background, glowing with exploding yellow stars. A few planets were scattered throughout the mask, orbiting in between the two mystic eyeholes. His eyes appeared as planets themselves, two blue moons peering out at me. The young man of twenty years seemed much older in person, given his large stature. He extended his hand. "It's a pleasure to meet you." He said with a laugh, "Say, how come your brother doesn't have to wear a mask?"

Eli heard James De Valle's comment and pointed to the mess of red, green, and black smeared across his face. "Face paint," he said with a shit-eating grin. "Fucking face paint."

CHAPTER
— 7 —

James De Valle reminded me of a sad hero from an old Western movie. He seemed to hold years of experience as if they were some great burden behind his bright blue eyes, as if he had seen too much, too soon. I asked him if he was enjoying the evening, and he nodded in compliance, running a hand through his wavy dark brown hair. James De Valle didn't say much, and I respected him for this; there is only so much a man can say before he is ultimately just talking to himself. He was witty when he wanted to be, and we shared some laughs, as Lucia made sure to keep pouring shot after shot. Eventually James and I were deep in conversation about storytelling. We had just drafted the outline of a novel, on the spot, and I was looking forward to writing it when I found the time. And I even explained the *Bad Dharma* to him a bit.

This novel was to be a modern-themed story about a musician (based on James De Valle) who falls down on his luck until he finds salvation in a beautiful Christian woman. When they meet, she is playing guitar on a street corner, and he starts to sing along; their chemistry is unrivaled. Together they travel across the country playing songs to small crowds and sleeping in his van when they can't afford decent lodging. One day, after eating some magic mushrooms, the man has a hallucinogenic dream. During his trip, a man who he presumes is Jesus Christ but is actually a street bum approaches him and tells him to kill the woman who has saved him. The man loves this woman, but she has taught him to always follow the Lord. So, one evening after they eat a nice meal at a small Americana restaurant, the man walks his love down a deserted alleyway. She tells him that dinner was lovely, and he tells her that he loves her very much. As they begin to kiss the man slides a small knife out of his back pocket. He then unbuttons her blouse and starts kissing her neck. She tilts her head toward the moon and closes her eyes. As the moonlight washes over her, her pleasured smile slowly fades into a grimace, and she falls to her knees. The man pulls the small knife from her back and touches the wound with his fingers. He holds her head with his dirty palms and sings to her sweetly as she bleeds out in a deserted Oklahoma alleyway. The man continues to tour, singing sad songs about the love he lost, though never once feeling a bit of remorse. The details weren't exactly set, but I planned on writing it sometime. James thought it could be turned into a good film as well.

Our collaboration ended abruptly, as the music stopped and a portly man—none other than Donald M. Humphrey, red-faced and tipsy—stood on a chair. He was supporting himself with his cane, which rested on a coffee table in the center of the room. He was holding a glass of champagne in his other hand. He started by thanking Eli and me for hosting the event. The crowd, without any hesitation, turned toward the bar and clapped a loud applause. *How did they know?* I thought. At the end of his speech, he announced a very large donation to the Chrysanthemum Foundation. He also announced that he would be running for mayor and asked for the gathering's support. This announcement was met with cheers of approval. I raised my glass as well. Donald M. Humphrey was a good man and he had my support.

The music started playing again, and I felt a tug on my sleeve. It was the olive-skinned beauty from before! With one hand on her hip and the other extended forward, she bowed and asked for a dance. I, of course, accepted. With the piano in full roar, I placed a hand on her lower back, feeling the silk of her dress as I dug my nails slightly into her flesh.

Walking to the center of the dance floor, I stopped briefly to shake Donald M. Humphrey's hand. I told him he had my support and planted a hard slap on his back. He started to say something, but my dance partner took my hand and tugged me farther into the crowd. As we started to dance I could see how truly beautiful she was. I held her hand and spun her in circles as her dark brown hair spiraled behind her like a top. Her hands were small and fit nicely in mine. Her eyes were dark and exotic. Her body was slim, and she knew how to move it in just the right way. After we had been dancing for a while, I sunk my face into the side of her neck, smelling a perfume equally as sweet as the roses scattered throughout the estate. I asked my partner for her name, but she told me it didn't matter, she was from Oregon and would be gone in the morning. But I persisted and she said if I liked I could call her Juliet, so I called her corny instead.

We danced close for what seemed like hours, and eventually she whispered in my ear, "Hey, Mr. Fox, would you like to go somewhere private?" And with her hand in mine we cut through the crowd, stopping at the bar briefly to joke with Lucia as she poured us all another drink.

"You be nice to James, now!" Lucia cooed as we pulled away.

"James?" she asked.

"Yes," I said.

She bit her lip playfully and said, "I thought your name was Mr. Fox?"

"You know who I am," I replied, pushing her along the wall while sliding my hands up and down the silk on her back.

The ballroom noise turned faint as we moved down the lower west hallway. I pushed open the tall wooden doors and we entered the library study, where we wasted no time in climbing up into the tree house.

In the tree house, she held my hand. I felt my body pushing against hers, pressing her into the wooden wall, and I reached down the side of my torso until I touched my hip and felt the cold silver in my hands. I drew Victoria's sword and rested it atop her right shoulder blade. With a flick of the wrist, the silk dress fell to the floor, a small trickle of blood dripping down the side of her arm. I did not apologize. I leaned forward and placed my mouth over the small cut. She stood speechless for a second, and then practically tackled me, pushing me back hard onto the wooden floor. When it was over, her mask was still on and so was mine. I felt her heart with my hand, and it was beating rapidly, like the footsteps of a young runaway.

We shared a cigarette, which she lit after reaching into my vest pocket for the lighter. We talked about her favorite bands, authors, films, and actors. She was a big James De Valle fan, and I told her he was a personal friend, and if she told me her *real name* I would introduce them. She told me that if she did, she would feel too close to me. She then placed a salmon-pink pill in my hand. She had told me earlier that she didn't understand the *Bad Dharma*, but the pills in her hand told me she did.

"Let me guess, queens are pink," I said.

"Nines." She laughed. "The nines are pink, and I always bet the nines," I heard her say as she walked her fingers across the center of my heaving chest.

"Always bet the nines!" I shouted, thinking of the drifter at the track who bet on Sal's Salvation. The wood ceiling inside of the tree house began to spin. As I sat up and started to speak, Juliet placed a finger to my lips. "Shhhhhh!" she whispered. The study doors creaked open and two men, one tall and one short, burst inward. They quickly closed the doors behind them. The taller man pushed the shorter, fatter one against the wall. At first I thought they were fighting. Looking closer, I noticed they were caught in a rather warm embrace, tongue in tongue.

Juliet dug her hand into my thigh in shock. We swallowed the salmon pills together, watching intently. I thought we should look away, but neither of us could, until something knocked me flat to the tree house floor. The salmon-pink pill was a downer; my mind began to spin in a chemical swirl. Juliet's head was resting on my hollow chest, and together we looked out through the railing of the tree house. The two men were aggressively intertwined. It was difficult to look elsewhere, and I felt ashamed for watching. After ten minutes or so, the men pushed away from each other, straightening their tuxedos and flattening their ruffled hair.

At that very moment, a cloud, which had previously stood between the moon and the study's large bay window, was blown aside. The wind came creeping through the open window, brushing nicely against my sweat-covered face. The breeze felt rather nice, but I never wanted the wind to blow, and I really wished it hadn't, because when the cloud moved away from the moon, a light came through the window and exposed James De Valle and Donald M. Humphrey exiting the library study together. Donald M. Humphrey once again at a disadvantage, hobbling behind due to his bum leg.

With a defining slam, the heavy doors closed and the two men were gone. I channeled my energy, craning my neck to look into Juliet's chocolate eyes, but the cool breeze had closed them. I placed a hand on her silver mask and started to pull it back, hoping to catch a glimpse of who she was. Something told me to stop. I pulled the edge of the mask back down and closed my eyes. I never wanted to see what was behind that mask. I placed my head back down on the wood floor and fell into a deep, teeth-grinding sleep. In my dream, I was back in the same grocery store where I had my mental breakdown, except this time every aisle in the store was labeled with a big red 9. In a panic, I turned down the canned foods section and started to run, except I could never reach the end of the row, and the shelves on either side of me began to grow into a stadium of people who were all shouting, "YOU GOT STUCK LUCK!" I told them to stop but they wouldn't listen.

Behind me I could hear the pounding of hooves slowly beating like war drums. At first, the sound was just a formidable buzz, and I ran with all my might, never once looking back as the people kept shouting. Eventually, the pattern of beating hooves grew louder, more detailed and intricate, each hoofbeat clapping and dispelling deafening echoes across the linoleum. Terrified and weak with vibration, I fell to the side of the aisle just in time to see the first horse pass. Time stood still for a brief second as the shirtless jockey turned and cocked a queer smile, just long enough for me to recognize the man from the racetrack—the man who had bet on Sal's Paradise. His gut bounced in slow motion as he rode along bareback. Then, as if someone had flipped fast-forward, the rest of the horses furiously flew past, and he was gone. After I was deflated and huddled on the linoleum, the floor broke open and swallowed me whole. I spun into a terrible darkness, but the voices still followed me until I woke up at 4 A.M. and instantly threw up off the side of the tree house. Juliet was gone. I slept peacefully for the rest of the night.

Eli Winston Buffalo and Lucia Lethridge would be almost inseparable for the next week, spending most of their time inside the estate as the cold weather had returned to the Tired Coast. Most of their time was spent in Eli's bed. However, they were fighting at that moment. Eli had stumbled home at four in the morning the previous night with lipstick on his collar and booze on his breath. Neither of them trusted each other, but more important, neither of them trusted themselves. So the following day, when Lucia had gone, it was most likely not a surprise to anyone except Lucia herself. She left this note pinned neatly to my bedroom door:

James,

It is with much sadness that I inform you of my sudden departure to San Francisco. Eli has become too unbearable at the moment, though I fear that I may love him. Sara will be accompanying me on an avocado truck that leaves this afternoon, she has a loft in San Francisco. I will be staying there for a while. I have already secured the arrangements with a tenant at the market so there is no need to insist on any other form of travel. I still regret not having introduced the two of you and that is why I am requesting you to contact me if you ever make it up North. I am not sorry for kissing you on the beach that day.

Good-bye, Peter.
Lucia

I set the letter on my desk and turned down the East Hall to find Eli. The kiss was the least of my worries after what I had witnessed that night with Juliet in the tree house. As I approached Eli's quarters, it was obvious by the crumpled wad in the hallway he had gotten a letter of his own. I thought it best to leave him alone. He knew that Lucia was a drifter and that she would do what drifters do and leave. He knew that he was to blame for his unfaithful tendencies. And he knew too well that Lucia and he were "not meant to be" in the traditional sense. Though it was obvious, as I looked through the narrow opening in his door, that he was reeling with the best of them. The bottle of Jack Daniels placed on his nightstand wouldn't make him feel better, but it probably wouldn't make him feel any worse. Hell, I felt like having a drink myself. Perhaps Sal Paradise was right—boys and girls in America have had such a sad time together.

CHAPTER
— 8 —

The crowd snarled as Rudy Hayes approached the batter's box, kicking a cloud of dust over home plate and turning once toward the opposing dugout to deposit an impressive amount of tobacco spit in their direction. The Tired Coast Admirals were in last place for the sixth straight year. The Admirals had lost their last seventeen games, and most of the crowd was out to heckle the home team. The Admirals' stadium, which was appropriately nicknamed "The Battle Field," seated only four thousand fans, and they were starting to get rowdy as the team's struggles continued. There was a delay in between the third and fourth innings, as fans started to throw debris onto the field. This was a familiar and welcoming environment for the Kentucky Cool Hawks, who were not a great team in their own right, sitting only one spot above the Admirals in the AAA baseball standings.

"Gotta love minor league baseball," I said to the portly man behind the concession stand as he handed me two cups of Bud Light. "Ah, screw it," I said, turning toward two Admirals faithful behind me in line. "What do you guys want?"

The two young men looked startled but wasted no time in responding, "Uh, beer?"

"This one's from Rudy Hayes," I said as I handed them the beers. "He says next year is going to be a heck of a lot better."

I made my way down to the grandstand toward my seat behind home plate. Hayes was down in the count, two strikes to one ball. A few drops of rain began to fall, and I watched as the drops plopped into the beer. The next pitch came in wild, almost hitting Hayes as he lurched away from home plate just in time. The crowd whooped and hollered, heckling Hayes, a few of them shouting, "Take one for the team!" The Cool Hawks pitcher punched his hand in his glove and looked toward the sky as if the slight moisture had caused him to lose control of the ball.

The count was even at two and two when I slid into my seat, passing a beer to Eli. He quickly took a sip and placed it in a cup holder. Eli was decked out in Admirals gear, a huge fan in his own right, though he never really seemed to enjoy baseball that much. I suppose he just liked the concept of being a fan.

"Let's go, Hayes, get a knock—here we go, buddy!" Eli shouted, removing his tan Admirals cap, which had a large burnt-orange "A" embroidered in the center. He had the matching tan jersey with the same burnt-orange trim and slanted navy lettering down the center that read "T.C. Admirals." It was quite possible Eli was the drunkest fan in attendance and the only one who actually wanted to see Hayes hit the ball. The rest of the crowd seemed to revel in the glorious disaster the Admirals' season had become.

Crackkkkkkk.

Hayes hammered the next pitch down the left-field line. The crowd jumped to their feet, and then subsequently fell back down as the ball landed foul. Eli almost had a heart attack in his excitement. He was still standing with his hands over his head by the time the rest of the stadium had settled back into their seats. "Alrightttt, here we go, Hayeseee, he's gonna give ya something now!" He shouted, picking up his cup. He pounded his beer and briefly looked over at me as if to say, *we've got this*. Rudy Hayes dug his feet into the dirt and readied himself for the next pitch. Eli dropped his empty cup and began to clap his hands.

The Cool Hawks pitcher glanced toward second base and then turned to face Hayes at home plate. He shook off a few signals from the catcher. Eventually he found one that he liked and he nodded his head. He reared back with all of his God-given might and hurled the ball, much to the crowd's delight, straight into the back of Rudy Hayes. Hayes hit the dirt but was not down for long. He got up seemingly unfazed and started to jog down the first-base line. Somewhere between home plate and first base, Hayes rerouted toward the pitcher's mound and planted a right hook into the side of the pitcher's head, knocking him out. The crowd roared. Both dugouts cleared, and the players met in a titanic clash at the pitcher's mound. Hayes still towered over the fallen Cool Hawk pitcher like a heavyweight champion. It was at the exact moment when the two minor league teams collided that the purple sky erupted and rain began to fall heavily. Eli buried his face in his hands as the rest of the stadium teemed with life, imitating Hayes's epic knockout blow.

I had to practically drag Eli out of the stadium. He was wasted and caught in the *samsara* that is minor league baseball. He was still down and out over Lucia's departure. I had thought an Admirals game would cheer him up. Guess not.

Usually, Eli could withstand any sort of beating the Admirals took. "I'll tell ya, James, that young Puerto Rican kid, Andres Cruz, he can play. You see him dive for that ball in center? A half an inch closer he would have had it!" he'd say with the utmost optimism. Now he was reduced to the mumbling of unintelligible cusswords tossed over my shoulder—as if there were such things as intelligible cusswords.

On the street, I waved for a taxi with my right hand, having little success with Eli cumbersomely draped over my left shoulder. Eventually a skinny white man with a goatee stopped his taxi. The driver was probably in his late sixties and looked like a decent guy. I tossed Eli into the back, and he landed in a heap, sprawling out window seat to window seat. I gave the driver an extra twenty to see that Eli made it into the house safely. Eli would be alright from there.

It had been two weeks since my last appointment with the Doctor, and it was time to see him again. I was short on my prescription after giving some to Eli and the waiter from The Gull. Over the last week I had to reduce my dosage to two pills a day instead of three. I felt fine.

The game had let out an hour early so I had time to kill before my appointment. I looked at the rain-delay voucher they had given me as I exited the stadium. Disgusted, I handed it to a kid in an Admirals cap.

Admiral fans had started to pour out in droves behind me. The rain was coming down harder as I started away from the stadium. My eyes caught a heavy man leaning against a lamppost. The man was lazily motioning for a taxi in between drags of his cigarette, his gut protruding outward in a distinguished and seemingly familiar way. The slimy feeling of déjà vu crept over me. I watched as a cab zipped up to the curb. The shirtless man turned his back to me, and I realized then that this was *the man*, the man I had sworn to befriend months ago, the man who had sold me his shirt at the track, and I'll be damned if he was shirtless again. Yes, I was certain it was the man who had "stuck luck," the man who "always bet nines," the man who was so wonderfully free, and the man who bet on Sal's Salvation against all odds.

I stepped forward to get a better look, but a family with a stroller pushed me back into the emerging crowd. I could barely make out my Buddha pulling all of himself into a city cab. The family passed and I began to push my way through the swarm of people. Before I knew it, I was running.

Weaving in and out of Admiral fans, I ran like a dancing gazelle. I found legs I never knew I had and then quickly lost them. I felt my stomach cramp, full of beer and beef jerky. Luckily the cab had stopped at a red light not too far away. I put my head down and painfully pushed toward the approaching intersection.

In a fit of desperation, I lurched off the curb prematurely and collided with a passing peanut vendor, toppling his cart. Peanuts flew everywhere as I fell into the oil-slicked street, landing flat on my stomach parallel to the stopped taxi. I reached an arm upward and started to beat on the cab's passenger door as a crowd slowly gathered around the fallen vendor. I looked up pitifully as the window rolled down and I saw, much to my disappointment, Bud Hawlings, the Admirals' general manager; he was not my man. Bud looked down at me, drunk and shirtless, in the back seat of the cab. He started to laugh, and with a smirk he lit up a fat cigar and told the cabbie to beat it when the light turned green.

Humiliated and out of breath, I got up and sheepishly handed the peanut vendor a twenty-dollar bill for the peanuts I had wasted. The man scowled at me as he took the money. He started to kick at the pigeons that had swarmed his fallen cart. The family that had cut me off with their stroller arrived at the intersection. As they passed, the little boy in the stroller pointed at the pigeons and said, "Look, Momma, birds!" The boy's father, who was pushing the stroller, looked at the peanut vendor condescendingly and made a rude comment. I turned the corner and ducked into a Coffee Bean as the two men began to argue. I ordered a large tea. I thought I asked for green but I wasn't sure.

I pressed my face against the window and watched as a heavy-set lady unsuccessfully attempted to use a newspaper as an umbrella, and behind her, a homeless man was drawn into a coughing fit outside a convenience store. *We've all got "stuck luck,"* I thought.

The lady was pulling a small black-and-white spotted dog along with her that seemed to have no problem with the rain. The dog repeatedly attempted to pounce on its reflection in the oil-slicked street, his little paws breaking the mirror-like surfaces of the city puddles. In the dog's most reckless attempt to catch what he thought was another small Dalmatian, the small puppy wrapped its leash around a light pole. His owner was almost brought to the ground in what would have undoubtedly been a large thud. Furious, the woman untangled the leash and tried to kick the puppy. The little dog reacted quickly, and this time his owner did in fact fall down to the asphalt with a resounding thud. Red-faced and completely drenched, the woman crossed the street. She made her way toward the Coffee Bean. The little dog pranced happily behind her, his head held high and tail a-wagging. When she reached the café entrance, the fat lady rolled the newspaper she had been using as an umbrella and struck the unsuspecting dog across its snout. Ironically the dog scampered underneath a nearby newsstand. The woman tied the leash to the side of the stand and pushed open the café doors, exposing the warm interior to the harsh elements outside. I finished my tea, which was green after all, and exited the café just as Cruella Deville was placing her order of a large double frap no whip, who the fuck cares.

The little dog was still under the newsstand as I stepped out onto the sidewalk. Only his tiny nose was visible. I placed my hand to the wet pavement in front of the stand. The dog's nose twitched curiously. Sensing I was a friend, the dog slowly exposed its spotted head, and I turned my palm upward for him to lick, but he went for my face, causing me to stumble back onto the sidewalk.

I laughed and I checked his collar for a name, but all I found was a tag-less brown leather band hanging loosely around his spotted neck. "Hmmm, what's your name, buddy?" I asked the dog, really just a puppy, who just tilted his head to the side. I placed my hand on its tiny head and scratched behind his perked ears, causing his tail to beat against the metal newsstand. The woman whose dog it was appeared to be boisterously talking on her phone inside the café. She was drawing stares from a young couple that had sat down in the window booth I had vacated. I reached into my back pocket and was delighted to find I still had some beef jerky left over from the ballgame. I tore a small piece and stuck it in my mouth, sucking the peppered flavoring off the dried meat. I lowered my hand halfway to the sidewalk, and the little dog jumped to take the jerky. He retreated back under the newsstand.

Underneath the sidewalk's overhang, I lit a cigarette, striking my lighter a few times before it produced an adequate flame. With my back against the window, I pushed heavy breaths of tobacco out into the approaching night. I noticed the spotted dog had reappeared and was looking up at me with some sort of strange admiration. I took a seat next to him on the sidewalk, and he rested his head on my thigh. In a moment of complete lack of judgment, or perhaps in a moment of utter brilliance, I untied the Dalmatian and tucked him underneath my warm flannel. Looking once up and down the deserted sidewalk, I crushed my cigarette against the sole of my boot and tossed it into a nearby trash can. Inconspicuously and without notice, the two of us slipped undetected into the night.

The dim streetlights outlined the falling rain but not the oncoming night, and in half a block the café was no longer visible. The tiny dog poked its head out from under my shirt collar and licked my face. Two blocks later we found shelter underneath a bus stop. The stop featured a large advertisement for Admirals Baseball. The ad starred none other than Rudy Hayes. He was dressed as a wizard, and he was holding a baseball bat instead of a wand. The post read: "COME SEE THE MAGIC! ADMIRALS BASEBALL."

The bus approached, clinking and clunking through the rain, coughing up black fumes like a sick smoker. I, once more, tucked the spotted puppy under my shirt. This time I buttoned my flannel all the way up to make sure he went unnoticed. I boarded the bus and headed toward the rear. Once seated two rows from the back and out of the driver's sight, I loosened my flannel shirt and allowed the Dalmatian to poke its head out for some fresh air. Afraid that the bus's littlest passenger might get motion sickness, I opened a window, and together we headed to the office of Doctor Henry P. Whitehouse, rain splattering on our indifferent faces.

No one seemed to mind the dog's presence, though I wasn't surprised. Most people on public transport tend to keep to themselves. Unfortunately, the few who do get in your business are most likely either high on something or devastatingly boring. I do my best to stay away from both types of people. High strangers can be dangerous and boring all at the same time; I suppose they're the worst. I once saw a man get beaten real badly on a trolley in San Francisco.

CHAPTER
— 9 —

The bus stopped a block away from the Doctor's office. I exited in a hurry as the little dog began to kick and claw underneath my flannel shirt. I knew it would be a challenge getting the puppy into the building; pets weren't allowed, and the doorman had never liked me. I spilled a cup of coffee in the lobby once, and he couldn't seem to let it go. Bruno Casey told me it was because the man had an obsessive-compulsive disorder—a condition that caused him to crave cleanliness. Bruno told me he had other quirks, too. Supposedly, every five minutes to the hour, he would exit through the side door and circle the block three times before coming back to his post. "Like clockwork," Bruno had said. "Every five to the hour. I'll show you sometime. When he leaves we can steal his porno magazines."

Approaching the building, I checked my watch. It read 7:53 P.M. I tucked behind a Dumpster in the alley and glanced at the side door. I needed Bruno to be right for once in his miserable life. A minute passed as the rain continued to soak through my clothes, and I could feel the little dog shaking against my stomach. I couldn't leave him out in the rain. Another minute passed; it was exactly five to the hour. The door did not open. My heart sunk. *Had the fat lady already informed the police of her missing pup?* I thought. *Is this why the doorman was staying loyal to his post?* I was about to throw up from anxiety when the side door kicked open and the doorman exited the alley. "Fucking loon!" I whispered to the dog, "We're saved."

I was hoping to ride with Mary Ann Lewis for a few floors. I saw no sign of her in the lobby, so I waited to press the elevator button. A few minutes passed and I checked my watch again. It read 7:57 P.M. I started to pace a bit. I took the dog out from beneath my shirt and placed him on the floor. The little dog sensed my nervousness and took a shit in the lobby. I looked at my watch and then back at the shit. Beads of sweat began to form on my forehead. 7:58 P.M. The doorman would be back any second. I looked toward the street and held my breath; I could see a figure approaching in the night.

My heart stopped. And then began to beat rapidly as I saw a sleek figure with a large red umbrella approaching. I could barely make out Mary Ann Lewis's yellow rain boots. I pressed the elevator button and the doors opened with a jerk. I grabbed the puppy and pulled us inside before Mary Ann Lewis had a chance to press her boots on the lobby's marble floor.

"Hold the elevator, please!" called a soft voice as the sound of frantic footsteps resonated through the lobby.

The little Dalmatian let out a nonthreatening bark in response. I noticed he was still shivering.

"Hey," I said, looking down at the little troublemaker between my feet. "I told you to bite Steve. Remember, the stuffy guy in a suit? I told you all about him on the way over. If you're going to—"

My scolding was cut short as Mary Ann Lewis stepped into the tiny space. "Puppy!" she squealed.

Mary Ann Lewis was late again. At the time I didn't know a whole lot about her, though I desperately wanted to. I knew that she introduced herself as Mary Ann Lewis. I also knew that she worked nights as a secretary for a doctor, whose name I couldn't remember, on the seventh floor. That was about it.

I was certain she knew very well who I was. My face had been plastered all over magazine racks, newspapers, and the local TV news the week we met, most of the headlines read, "Buffalo Heir Insane?"

When we first met, I was really strung out, skinny and pale, just reemerging from a nervous breakdown. My right arm was broken and we couldn't shake hands. Not that it mattered, I could hardly bare to look at her. She was brimming over the top with happiness, and I was trying to stay afloat. She asked me what I did for a living, and all I could say was "Nothing, I suppose." She was referring to my occupation, and I wasn't really occupied by much anymore. And I didn't really do much by way of enhancing the fortune Charles David Buffalo had recently left me. That would have been very hard for me to do, considering I was not blessed with stellar business instincts. I could write, though I had never derived any serious income from it. And I hadn't written anything for three years. Something happened that left my mind filled with a million blank pages.

My only problem with the headlines that came out in the week I broke down, consequently the week I met Mary Ann Lewis, was not the questioning of my sanity but the failure to mention my own existence as an author—not a single footnote. Simply my existence was characterized as an "heir."

I had written a few short stories when I was younger, which Doris submitted to *Discovery Kids*, and a total of four were published in the magazine by the time I was twelve. I had also written a grand total of two mid-length novels, both completed before I turned twenty-one. The first was published in 2007 and titled, *The Seven Dreams*. The second novel was passed up by the publishers, so I had to print it myself, which was rather embarrassing, though I did sell three thousand copies. Still, I do not speak much of this novel.

The Seven Dreams is rather good, or at least so I am told. Personally, I believed everything I have ever written is a flaming piece of shit. I was working on reversing this "type of think." *The Seven Dreams* is about a young boy who gets trapped inside a sequence of seven dreams. Each dream takes place in a different world but ultimately the same universe. The fourth dream takes place in the black space of the universe and is the grimmest of the seven. The boy ages sequentially with each dream, eventually forgetting that he is actually a youth who has fallen asleep under a shady crab apple tree in Sioux Falls, North Dakota. The most riveting dream is probably the sixth. The boy, who is now a man of one hundred and twenty-five, wakes up on a planet called Armidius. He is so old at this point that he no longer cares about the shattered and corrupt universe he has discovered in his previous five dreams. The planet Armidius is inhabited with large marshmallow-like creatures called Aminodorphes—Dorphies for short. Dorphies have cat-like faces but no real arms and legs, essentially floating about in Armidius's atmosphere like stray balloons caught in God's jet stream. Dorphies are completely in line with the ways of the universe and have little thinking other than the feeling of move-ment. Too old to walk, he fastens himself to the back of a Dorphie, whom he names Mackenzie. Assuming he will die on the back of Mackenzie, the old man surrenders himself to a simple existence at the whim of the Dorphie's moment. The old man experiences a spiritual existence greater than any divine figure could provide or any man could understand. This dream is the dream that ultimately allows the boy to wake up, leading into the seventh dream, which is essentially reality. When the boy wakes up, he has already lived a lifetime inside his mind and has no desire to be anywhere other than where he is at the present. He simply grabs an apple from the tree and places his back against its trunk, sitting there for the next one hundred twenty-five years in complete harmony.

CHAPTER
— 10 —

As the elevator doors closed, I bit my lip and wrestled with my collar. I couldn't help but wonder if Mary Ann Lewis read. I ran with this thought for a bit until I imagined a scenario where the two of us made love in a library after hours. I felt like a creep. And as we ascended I cursed myself for smoking.

By the time we passed the second floor I had not spoken a single word. Mary Ann Lewis did not notice. She was playing with the tiny Dalmatian at the moment. I pressed tightly against the wall, ashamed of my silence, yet very much amused. I was soaking wet and a puddle was forming at my feet, whereas Mary Ann Lewis was completely dry, unfazed by the downpour. She always carried an umbrella. I had noticed this about her. Even on sunny days she would bring an umbrella to work. One would assume someone who was prepared enough to carry an umbrella on a sunny day would undoubtedly have their act together. That was not the case with Mary Ann Lewis.

As we passed the third floor, she began to frantically rifle through her purse and displaced several objects, including, much to my surprise, a fresh package of cigarettes. *What a relief!* I thought, and I started to relax a bit. Yes, how fitting that the seventh-floor secretary smokes. I imagined her trying to conceal the fact from her boss, opening a window in the ladies' room, displacing the faintest trail of smoke. Afterward, carefully splashing perfume on her wrist to cover up the evidence.

Mary Ann Lewis stopped digging through her purse and pulled out a small oval-shaped container. She began to apply blush to her cheeks, which were already decidedly rosy. She finished and tore off her yellow-knit beanie. The wool hat spiraled through the air and landed squarely on the puppy's head, covering his big eyes. I laughed as the dog let out a frustrated whimper.

"I am sorry," Mary Ann Lewis said to me, forcing a smile. "One second...," she said, pulling her hair into a bun. She failed to capture one thin curl of dirty blonde hair, and it fell perfectly across her forehead. I wanted to tell her she looked nice, but I didn't.

Mary Ann Lewis looked at the dog and giggled, curling her soft pink lips, which were lighter in color than usual, given the cold weather. Time seemed to slow, and with a huff, she blew the hair that had escaped her bun out of her face. She bent down to pick up the cigarettes she had dropped, and when she did, she adjusted the cap on the dog's head so that his entire spotted face became visible again.

"Waaaaa-laaa!" she exclaimed as time sped up again.

The puppy stood there, overwhelmed with his first real taste of dignity, wearing the hat as if it were his crown. The world, as he knew it, was bound to be his kingdom. At that moment I decided to name the tiny Dalmatian "King."

"His name is King," I said as Mary Ann Lewis stood up. She smiled and said that it was a nice name. I looked at the cigarettes in her hand and asked her to smoke. She smirked and said, "I would, except smoking is for the damned." She wiggled the pack of cigarettes in my face and shrugged, smiling like a condescending schoolteacher. "These are for my boss. He's a doctor on the seventh floor," she said, sliding the pack back into her purse. "I am quitting today and figured I could bring the man one more package of coffin nails."

"Why are you quitting?" I asked nonchalantly, trying to sound like I didn't care, even though I did.

"Well, I am not sure you would understand," she said, leaning closer so that I could smell her vanilla perfume.

Mary Ann Lewis started to speak and then paused for a second. She scrunched her nose tight, seemingly caught between thoughts or on the verge of unleashing a thunderous sneeze. She was still standing close to me in the elevator when we passed the sixth floor. Grasping her rosary necklace in her right hand, she massaged each of the wooden beads. I wondered what she had to repent. She then leaned even closer and whispered something I would never forget.

"It's all a bunch of shit, and you, my friend... ," she paused and patted my face. "Well, you, my friend, have a chance to make it out alive."

"Huh?" I croaked, clearly taken aback.

"The quacks in here are fucking worse than the patients they see." Mary Ann Lewis looked around the elevator as if we were being watched. "I know they're all the same on every floor! But you know that now, don't you, James?" she said, raising her voice from a whisper to a formidable buzz.

"I did not," I said as I eased back a step, glancing down toward my feet, not ready for whatever could be so disappointing.

Mary Ann Lewis did not hesitate in closing the gap I had formed.

"Dr. Henry Q. Winchester on the sixth floor is having an affair!" She grabbed the collar of my flannel, and I couldn't help but offer a sheepish grin, not fully sold on it. "His wife is certain of it. I rode with her in this same elevator two days ago!" She took one large gasp of air before sliding the rosary necklace back into her blouse. "Dr. Sara C. Goddard, also on the seventh floor, has three children. She had a fourth who died in an automobile crash last September. I sent her a card expressing my condolences, and she sent one back that said, 'At least it wasn't the smart one!'" Mary Ann Lewis started to laugh madly on the brink of hysteria.

"THE SMART ONE!" she screamed, causing King to jump up and dislodge the yellow beanie from his head.

"And finally, Dr. Richard L. Darling, my boss. I bring him cigarettes, but he doesn't—"

"Ding-Ding!" screamed the elevator.

The seventh floor had finally arrived, interrupting Mary Ann Lewis. However, she had not finished. Grabbing my arm, she pulled me out of the elevator and sat me down in a lobby chair next to a fake ivy plant and a lifetime's supply of *National Geographic* magazines. "Wait here!" she exclaimed.

CHAPTER
— 11 —

The rest was sort of a daze. I sat in the lobby with King while Mary Ann Lewis screamed obscenities at Dr. Richard L. Darling. I read half the cover article of the most recent *National Geographic*, titled "Evolution of the Royal Wedding Dress," and felt pretty enlightened about royal fashion. Whether I will ever find this information useful, I am not sure.

Mary Ann Lewis walked back into the lobby rather composed for someone who had just dramatically terminated herself. I lifted my eyes from the magazine just as she reached behind her head to release the tight bun she had woven minutes before in the elevator. Her hair fell cascading around her face and shoulders. She was free.

When she asked if I wanted to go for a walk under her red umbrella, I was already there. The Doctor would have to wait.

Mary Ann Lewis, King, and I took the stairs down to the first floor and snuck out the side door so that the doorman wouldn't see King. I explained to Mary Ann Lewis that the dog was stolen, and she seemed fine with this. "We will have to keep him hidden then," she said. I told her I was worried I would not be able to get King back into the building; the side door from which we exited had automatically locked behind us. "You worry too much," said Mary Ann Lewis. "I'll think of something." I could tell she was fond of the dog. Once we were outside on the street, I asked Mary Ann Lewis what Dr. Richard L. Darling had done. She simply smiled and told me softly, "It's all in the past now."

I was fine with the answer. Some things are better left unknown. *It's all clutter*, I thought, as we pushed into the night. The three of us huddled close under Mary Ann Lewis's large umbrella and took a stroll toward the city park. I listened intently as Mary Ann Lewis told me about the wonders of Jesus Christ. She spoke primarily of love and its healing powers. Essentially, I derived that Jesus Christ was love, and so was I. Mary Ann Lewis told me a story about her cousin in Santa Cruz who had recently started seeing a woman doctor similar to Richard L. Darling. He was only twelve when he first started on prescriptions a year before. He used to send Mary Ann Lewis colorful drawings of dinosaurs. Now he thinks dinosaurs are stupid and sits quietly in his room, never making a sound. I guess this is why she quit.

We discussed everything strangers should talk about to become properly acquainted, discussions ranging from cold remedies to her upbringing in Sun Valley, Idaho. Mary Ann Lewis told me that I should just call her Mary Ann. I wasn't sure how I felt about that. Not too long ago I had scolded Steve for calling her Mary Ann—I couldn't help but laugh. I then asked Mary Ann Lewis what her oldest memory was, and she told me it was Christmastime in Sun Valley. She was only three. Little Mary Ann Lewis was sitting in her mom's lap beneath the Christmas tree, which was lit with many colorful lights. The smell of pine and apple cider wafted through the air while snowflakes slowly painted the fence in the front yard the softest of whites. On the floor, a small train was circling the tree, her father the conductor. The train's tiny wheels made a jingling sound much like the sound of change bouncing in a Buddha's pocket.

Clink, clink, cllllliinkkkkkkk.

The train circled the tree, disappearing for a few seconds before reemerging. As the train turned the bend, her father would blow its horn, and she would giggle just as her father knew she would. The process would repeat. Each time the train would disappear for a few seconds, and then turn the bend, sounding its horn. Each time Mary Ann Lewis giggled. The best things in life are consistent. When things in the universe don't spin like they should, that is where the hurt is. I suppose that is why I hadn't written in years. It was a good first memory, and I told Mary Ann Lewis I was very glad she had shared it with me.

She then asked what my oldest memory was. I told her that I wasn't sure if it was an actual memory or a reoccurring dream that had started early in my childhood. We both ultimately agreed that it did not matter because a memory of a dream is still a memory, and childhood is pretty dream-like anyway. The memory or memory of a dream takes place at Sunday brunch in which everyone is dressed nicely, the women in beautiful dresses and the men in suits. I am outside on a dock with other children. An older girl tells me it's okay to put my feet in the water, and she places a hand on my shoulder to make sure I do not fall in. She then hands me half of a French roll, and we begin to toss crumbs to the family of ducks swimming in the lake. I am pretty sure it's a dream memory.

En route to the city park, Mary Ann Lewis decided to make a detour on Fifth Avenue.

"I just remembered something!" she said, sharply turning left down Pelly Street as I struggled to stay underneath the big red umbrella. Halfway down the street we stopped in front of an old office building that was about eleven stories high.

I followed Mary Ann Lewis around the side of the building, where she knocked a calculated three times on the back door of what I presumed was the first-floor lobby. A tall, bald man with circle-framed spectacles answered the door, and after a few seconds or so, he stepped into the alley, pulling his collar high to shelter his thin face from the downpour. He looked at me, then down at the dog for only a second before turning his hawk-like nose toward Mary Ann Lewis. He extended a hand outward, palm up, and then we all heard a horrific crunching sound followed by a car alarm.

The sound of colliding metal caused the man to jump backward a foot or so, and he looked nervously toward the street. Mary Ann Lewis snapped her fingers, and the man looked back at her. She handed the skittish man a crumpled wad of bills, and in return he gave her a small sandwich bag filled with what looked like dried sticks. She slid the bag into her purse. She then led King and me back to Pelly Street, where a traffic jam had formed, the result of a taxicab colliding with a dark-blue Escalade. A fit Hispanic police officer was running past the alleyway as we emerged back onto the sidewalk. He almost collided with the three of us and probably would have if it were not for Mary Ann Lewis's bright-red umbrella.

"Watch yourself, Officer!" she said.

No one on the Tired Coast really knew how to drive in the rain, as evidenced by the Escalade's crumpled front fender. Even the cabbies had trouble. Oh the irony in everyday subtleties we take for granted.

When we reached the park, Mary Ann Lewis sat down on a bench facing the lake. There were no ducks on the lake because of the rain. Not to get all Holden

Caulfield on you, but seriously, where do the ducks go when it rains? Regardless, I love watching rain fall on a body of water. So much movement, it's hard to pinpoint one specific raindrop that has more impact than the rest.

Mary Ann Lewis reached inside her purse and pulled out the bag the man had given her in the alley. "Have you ever taken mushrooms?" she asked me. I looked at the bag and told her I had not.

She smiled and slid the fungus back into her purse. As she did so, I noticed her left hand grazed the exposed portion of her rosary necklace that rested loosely on her collar. "Neither have I." She said after few moments of silence. "I have heard of people having spiritual experiences when they take them..." She paused, looking out at the grey lake. "I think I am due for one of those."

I looked out over water as well. I watched the white chops collide and disappear as the lake was filled with new water from the afternoon's leaky sky. *We could all use one of those moments*, I thought.

And as the rain began to fall a little harder, I couldn't help but think the heavens were crying for all of us. And after a few minutes of somewhat confusing and depressing silence, I wanted my pills. I looked at my watch and saw that it was already 8:29 P.M. "I should head back," I said. Mary Ann Lewis just nodded.

I stood up from the park bench and pulled my collar up to shelter my neck from the rain. With my hair pressed flat against my face in the rain, almost covering my eyes,

I decided to ask the question I had wanted to for so long. "What does Doctor Henry P. Whitehouse have to hide?" I said.

Mary Ann Lewis bit her lip, still looking out at the water. She pulled skinny headphones from her purse and placed the buds in her ears. She traced the cord from her ears to the center of her iPod and moved her thumb in a circular motion, eventually stopping and looking up at me. "Well, James, I suppose that the Doctor has...," she paused for a moment, the circular motion of her thumb coming to rest. "Well, James, he has, you."

"Muh... me?" I stuttered.

"Yes, you," she said.

"How so?" I asked, following her gaze out over the lake.

"Do you remember when we first met?" she asked, her voice calm and motherly. Without waiting for my answer, she added, "Well, I asked you what you did, James, and you said, 'Nothing.'"

"Mary Ann, I was—" I started to defend myself.

"Stop. Listen." She interrupted.

"You said, 'Nothing,' okay?"

"So, what's your goddamn point?" I said.

"I guess what I am trying to say is that, well, nobody does nothing. You're better than you think, James. People like you, and you can't see it." She said reaching into her purse. She pulled out a small paperback book. "Here!" She shoved the book into my chest. "Believe it or not, some people like you, so you shouldn't be an asshole and pretend that you're so cool and absent-minded and sick with unholy nothingness all the time!"

And with that Mary Ann Lewis and her bright-red umbrella disappeared into the rain. And I was left standing with a copy of *The Seven Dreams* in my hands, counting raindrops like disappearing women on the lake. *Yes*, I thought, *not one drop is more significant than the rest, but could that really be true?*

CHAPTER
— 12 —

"Mary Ann Lewis chews peppermint candies when she gets sick because she hates the taste of cough drops—I know this," I said turning dramatically toward the Doctor, "because I just spent the last half hour walking underneath her bright-red umbrella!"

I expected the Doctor to be happy for me; however, his ensuing silence told me otherwise. A puddle formed at my feet as I anxiously awaited his response. The fireplace was lit and the room smelled nice. The Doctor scribbled furiously in his journal and did not look up at me as the firelight flickered on his tense jawline. A kettle for tea was on the stove in the background, puffing out scattered clouds of steam as the water began to boil, not quite ready to scream.

I sat down on the floor next to King and let him chew a bit on the sleeve of my flannel. I had managed to sneak him past the doorman by placing him in a Macy's box I had found in the Dumpster. This was Mary Ann Lewis's idea. "There is a toy drive on the tenth floor," I said to the doorman as he scrubbed dog shit off the lobby floor. The man did not look up—he just scrubbed and scrubbed.

The excitement from my excursion with Mary Ann Lewis began to fizzle and flatten out into a dull and painful tension. The Doctor was clearly upset. A few more minutes of silence passed. Then the teapot's whistle sharply cut through the room, and King urinated on the carpet.

The Doctor got up and pulled the screaming kettle from the stove. He then sat back down and called for one of his assistants to clean up the mess. Much to my growing discomfort, Jody Eloise, the sweet mail girl, was the one who showed up with paper towels and a bottle of Resolve. How ironic. The Doctor didn't say a word; he simply pointed to the puddle on the carpet. I tried to mouth a "sorry," but I wasn't sure she noticed. The Doctor could care less about Jody Eloise. Leaning against his messy desk, he simply tossed his diamond-print scarf over his left shoulder and watched as she went to work. To the Doctor, it didn't matter that Jody Eloise was a sweet girl. To him she was just a mail girl who had a tendency to deliver the mail incorrectly.

The trash bin in the Doctor's office was full of mail addressed to Dr. Henry Q. Winchester, who worked on the sixth floor. Jody always got them confused, and the Doctor never bothered to return the mail. I wondered if Dr. Henry Q. Winchester's trash was filled with letters addressed to Dr. Henry P. Whitehouse.

The Doctor's walls had changed again, this time to an oak shade of maroon. I looked over at cute little Jody as she scrubbed away, and I wondered if she had to paint the walls as well. All the portraits had been removed except for one, a painting of a young boy standing in a field of California orange poppies.

"You're late, James, forty minutes late," the Doctor said as Jody exited the room. He lifted King from the floor with one of his wrinkled hands. "We only meet once every two weeks, and yet you make me wait?"

"Yes, I know. I must explain. You see, Mary Ann—"

"It's fine, James," he said shaking his head. The Doctor set King back down on the floor. He rolled up the sleeves of his light-blue cardigan and proceeded to pour the tea into the drinking china. "I just want you to take this seriously." He finished with a sigh.

"I take this seriously." I replied.

"Good," said the old man as he dropped two cubes of sugar into his tea with a plunk. As the steam billowed from the drinking china, he turned and said with the slightest flicker of remorse, "You're glowing."

The Doctor got up again before I had a chance to respond. The fire cracked as he removed a purple bottle from his pharmaceutical cabinet. My eyes lit up as he shook some pills out onto his desk. He sat back down and handed me a cup of tea. I took a sip and burnt my tongue. The Doctor smiled and then motioned toward the pills. "Now," he said, "tell me about the wonderful Mary Ann Lewis."

I grabbed three pills off the desk and swallowed them dry. I felt a sensation of calm creep over me. I had no problem telling the Doctor about my adventure with Mary Ann Lewis. He was sure to see what a good thing she was. I left out the part about the hallucinogenic mushrooms of course. And I felt as though he owed me an explanation for all the madness that had caused Mary Ann Lewis to quit. Dr. Henry Q. Winchester's affair and Sara C. Goddard's insensitivities were killing me. *How could they heal anyone?* I thought. I needed him to say that he was different.

When I finished, there was a strange sense of calm in the room, and I looked down and noticed King was asleep peacefully on the carpet. *How long had I been talking?* I thought. Then the Doctor spoke calmly. "Yes, what a shame about Dr. Winchester," he said, looking toward his trashcan. "I really do like his wife, Susan Winchester. I, in fact, was the one who encouraged her to act on her suspicions of adultery. And as for Sara Goddard, she went to Columbia with me and graduated with honors. However, James, you have to understand that some people don't have the faintest idea how to deal with any significant events in their own lives. Some people will always be better at telling others how to deal with things, and these people will never be able to cope with their own tragedies. When you do this, you see your own life as a regrettable comedy. I am afraid this is what has happened to Sara."

The Doctor circled the room, eventually taking a seat on the floor. He rested his head against one of his wooden medical cabinets. King woke up, and the Doctor motioned for the dog to sit beside him.

"So, what do you think it is I am hiding, James?" said the Doctor with conversational ease, petting the top of King's head. I could tell then that he wasn't going to tell me he was any different than his colleagues. I could feel his burning eyes as he looked right through me, his insides churning with anger.

"I don't know," I said, "but I want to start writing again."

"Ha! What did we just talk about, James?" the Doctor shouted. "We all know you have nothing to write about. Hell, you can't cope with anything real. You are no better than Sara Goddard. Your writing is only a cowardly way of prolonging fantasies that devoid you of any real substance. So much time goes into your writing and all you get in return is a goddamn broken arm and a father that cannot trust you! When you write, you turn your life into that regrettable comedy. You need to do real things, James. Like your father would have wanted."

Drawing one long match from his front shirt pocket, the Doctor dragged it slowly across the rich mahogany surface of his desk, back and forth, producing no flame. He continued to flirt with the match, twirling it in his long fingers, stroking the ruff of King's neck. King looked at me, and I could tell he was frozen. I under-stood. Finally, when the flirtation was over, the Doctor looked up and muttered, "James, James, what are we going to do with you?" and he snapped the match down along the edge of the desk producing one bright yellow flame.

CHAPTER
— 13 —

As the van pulled through the coastal pines, my face caught every scattered ray of light. I had little yearning to see the Doctor again. I had stopped caring about Charles David Buffalo's Last Will and Testament. Eli had no restrictions and could easily float me some cash while I figured things out. This of course meant that I was done with the pills. I had my last prescription in my backpack next to a journal for writing. Something good had happened after I left the Doctor's office that night, the night I walked under Mary Ann Lewis's big red umbrella for the first time.

In the back seat of the van, I examined the *Last Will and Testament of Charles David Buffalo*. I reread the same passage with little progress. I had not looked at the document since Charles David Buffalo's attorney had read it to me last year. Charles Buffalo's lawyer was a short man, very tan, with olive-oil eyes. He wore cheap cologne and slicked his jet-black hair tight behind his ears, making the veins on his forehead pop.

The passage he read to me while I sat patiently in my breakfast robe was Clause 3B.

Clause 3B.

Effective immediately upon the death of myself, Charles David Buffalo, James Reid Buffalo's trust is rendered void. In regard to James Reid Buffalo's inheritance such restrictions do apply. These restrictions come not as a punishment and these restrictions can only be seen as a helping hand from the wise and deceased. It is my wish that James make a full recovery from the plagues of his mind. He needs to cope with emotion logically. I entrust the first half of my fortune to James under the strict condition that he regularly visit and undertake the psychological services of the family friend, and entrusted aide, Doctor Henry P. Whitehouse, until he is deemed well, well enough to manage a large sum of money appropriately and responsibly, upholding my legacy.

That had been the most Charles David Buffalo had ever communicated with me. Fittingly it caused me to choke on my toast. I spit strawberry jam and sourdough clear across the table onto the face of Charles David Buffalo's lawyer. I could tell he was not amused. In fact, when he read the passage again, he said the words with such disdain that Eli almost "flattened his pointy nose."

My face grew warm. Yes, very warm. My face became cold as the light receded and it occurred to me that I was alone on this journey. I did not mind. It gave me time to contemplate what it meant to be well.

If I get some spare time, I would like to get my life together. These were the first lines I wrote in my journal, with messy handwriting, as the van hit some bumps along the road. I thought about my last session with the Doctor.

There will be no redemption in the togetherness, I scribbled underneath. I felt for my pulse and it was beating. I must have been well. The pattern repeated. I was warm, and then I was cold.

Fuck togetherness. I wrote just before I closed my journal and placed it back in my backpack.

The van hummed along. My face was warm, and then it was cold. I must have been well, though I had no idea how to interpret the words written and ultimately said by Charles David Buffalo in *Clause 3B*. For the moment, *Clause 3B* seemed to be as insignificant as a dog defecating on my front lawn; it was shit. I crumpled the photocopied *Last Will and Testament of Charles David Buffalo*, and let the wind take it outside of the van. I immediately felt bad for littering.

I started to feel a little anxious, so I reached into my bag and pulled my last canister of pills and dispensed two into my hand. The noise of the shaking pill bottle penetrated the van. I heard a male's voice come from the driver's seat, a voice as dangerous as a snake's rattle. The sound floated back and slithered into my left ear. "Hey, how 'bout you share some of those?"

I ignored the voice. There was no chance. I had only ten pills left, minus the two I ate for breakfast three hours earlier. I would have to ease off the pills slowly. So I swallowed two pills knowing full well a rapid withdrawal could be dangerous.

It's worth it, I thought, as my face grew warm again. I put the pills away. *I have a reason to be better now*, I thought.

Mary Ann Lewis smiled as sunlight filled the dimples of her cheeks. She was stretching, the tips of her fingers sprawling across the roof of the van, and then pulling back across her pulsating body. I could not find the energy to fully look into her blue eyes as I felt a hand slide across my lap.

"Stop, Mary Ann, wouldya!" I whispered playfully.

She began to giggle, as she ran her hand up and down my thigh, feeling the sensation of corduroy.

"Hey buddy, it's cool if you don't want to share your meds. I was just kiddin.' But do me a solid and snap a shot of Al for me?" The male voice interrupted our flirting. Al was the name of our recently adopted highway flower. I removed Al from the canteen I had been keeping him in and started to wrap my fingers around his bright green stem. This must have looked strange because everyone started to laugh. King had been asleep on the floor and he awoke.

"He is tripping so hard," Mary Ann Lewis said, as her blonde hair moved unpredictably in the wind. I smiled and nodded as we passed through the sweet-smelling California pines.

"Al really is the strangest of characters, real moody if you ask me. But there is something about him. I just can't find the words right now, but I am sure you understand. Anyway, snap a shot of him once we get back into the sunlight," said the voice. It occurred to me then that the voice was Eli's. I traced his words to the driver's seat like bread crumbs. I found my brother bearded and hunched over the VW steering wheel in the most peculiar way.

"No one is going to steal your wheel, Eli!" shouted Mary Ann Lewis. And we all busted up pretty good until it was hard to breathe. When the laughter stopped, Eli hunched back over the steering wheel and shot me a skeptical look. I slid back into the rear of the van and sat back down next to Mary Ann Lewis. We had all eaten the mushrooms she bought from the man with a hawk-like nose in the alley.

I focused on Al, the flower. It was breathing and so were we. I thanked him for being well. "Do you remember everything?" I whispered to the flower, which just swayed in the wind. I imagined his response to be "Why, what else could there be to remember than this right now... wait, uh, what was the question?"

"What the hell!" Eli yelled.

"Uh, yeah," I mumbled. "Just, uh, let me finish..."

Silence. I turned toward Al and told him, "This won't hurt a bit," and felt the shuttering of the lens vibrate through my hands. I laughed and whispered, "We will remember you."

I shifted my focus from the flower to Mary Ann Lewis. Her goddamn hair was dancing across the back seat of the van, occasionally brushing my face. King had jumped onto the padded back row and had nestled himself between the two of us. I started to pet his neck. My wandering mind circled back to *Charles David Buffalo's Last Will and Testament* again. Specifically the part in *Clause 3B* that stated, "... until he is deemed well, well enough to manage..." To me, wellness was living completely in the moment; too many sad things had happened in the past, whereas the future was too hard to conceive without worry or anxiety.

The Doctor loved the past. I remembered sitting in his office months back. "So, James," he had said. "Do you remember when you and Eli went camping with Doris in the San Bernardinos?"

"Uh, yeah, sure," I said.

"Well, do you?" he asked.

"Yeah, I remember," I muttered.

"Let's see, you were, ahhhhhh, thirteen?" he said.

"Yeah, that's right," I replied.

"Do you remember when you and Eli snuck away from camp down to the river while Doris was fixing breakfast?" he said.

"No," I lied.

"James, I know you do." He spoke sternly. "I have Doris's book, remember, *The Raising of Eli and James Buffalo: America's Reveling Youth*." He pulled the book out of his desk and shook it in my face.

"Yes, of course," I replied.

"Well, what happened at the river, James?" he asked.

"Listen, could we just drop it? I don't—" I said.

"You shot and killed your first buck! You became a man, James. But let's see what it says here... um... yes, on page seventy-six, I believe. Yes, here we are." The Doctor said before reading the following passage aloud:

> ...*James was distraught though he had provided us with dinner. Eli skinned the meat even though he was younger. James wouldn't look at the deer. Nor did he eat for the rest of the trip. That night I saw him crying by the river.*

"James! You became a man!" he yelled boisterously.

"I was thirteen," I mumbled.

"Your first kill! Providing a woman and your younger brother with food. A man, I say," the Doctor said with a smile.

"You always remember your first," I replied with lost sarcasm.

"But tears, James. Were you upset your father wasn't there?" The Doctor continued to ask questions in which he already knew the answers.

"I was upset I killed something so beautiful," I told him.

"Nonsense, you provided food. You became a man," he said, closing the book. "You became a man."

I was upset because I killed something beautiful— my innocence.

— 🐚 —

In the van, I fixed my eyes on the passing forest floor, which flew by in a leafy swirl of earthiness.

"Oh, James, why won't you look at me?" I heard Mary Ann Lewis say, her voice so womanly. "Does it pain you to see my face?"

"No, I like your face," I said. The mushrooms made me feel talkative. "There are just so many things equally beautiful and magnificently wonderful in this universe." I was having a revelation. "The fact is, dear, I see you in those tiny golden flowers on the hill there."

"Where?" Mary Ann Lewis said, looking out the window.

"There!" I yelled, pointing to the colorful hillside. "And I know I will see you in the ocean when we turn the bend here. I will see you in all of the tiny drops of water. I will see you there turning the Pacific turquoise, and I'll see you in the tiny particles of light that cause it to glimmer. This I know for certain... and I see you sitting beside me here in the van."

We started to kiss, the feeling of her tongue felt so foreign and strange in my mouth. After a minute or so we pulled apart. We rode in silence for a while, watching the glistening ocean come into view on the west side of Highway 101. Slowly, I felt as though I were being lifted from the van, floating in accordance with everything in some sort of great trance as we pulled along the warm California pavement.

"WHAT ARE YOU DOING?" Eli's voice penetrated my dreaming as I sunk back into the van.

Eli was looking back at me with tears in his eyes, one hand on the wheel. I looked down and I noticed that Al has been reduced to nothing, just a green stem with no petals. "Whhhhy, I maaa-mean how could you?" he stammered as tears slid down his bearded face. I hadn't known Eli and Al were that close.

As the salty air spiraled through the van, Eli looked back at me with his mouth agape. Time appeared to have stopped for him. I had heard of people getting emotional during mushroom trips. I'd never really understood it. I wanted to throw up. No, seriously. I was going to vomit. Must have been the fungus.

I collected my mind. The nausea passed. To no one's surprise, I found myself speechless. Before I could construct a coherent sentence, I felt Eli's embrace on my shoulder. He sniffed, "It's alright, buddy. I know ya' didn't mean nothing by it." He was right, I really didn't.

The van swerved dramatically, and Eli turned his attention back toward the wheel, once again hunching over in focus. I noticed Mary Ann Lewis was crying too but for a different reason—she had just had the spiritual moment she was looking for. She began to kiss the beads of her rosary.

I didn't know what to make of any of it. I wrote the following in my journal once everyone had calmed down:

December 2011,

I ate mushrooms for the first time today and I accidentally killed our highway flower named Al. I really didn't mean to. And I guess it didn't really matter because he was dead the moment we plucked him from the ground. I didn't want to say that, though, since everyone was already upset. Eli and Mary Ann both cried, but for different reasons that seemed equally strange to me. I was feeling sentimental myself, and I think the others could tell because I felt like we were all one, and when they calmed down I calmed down as well.

The mushrooms were supposed to give us something spiritually, though I am not sure I liked them; maybe spirituality is the last thing I need at the moment. I am withdrawing from MRX2857. I am nervous and content at the same time. Perhaps I am content with the nervousness, if that makes sense.

More importantly, I have come to a revelation that my eyes tend to speak for me at times, yours do too. I should probably learn to keep mine closed. My eyes are tired as hell. Yes, I should close my eyes and start opening my mouth. I should start spitting deception like snake venom. Eyes can be devastatingly honest, whereas words can be controlled and regulated, honest at times but fictitious by design—when the great Buddha tells you that words are nothing more than labels, know that he is dead wrong.

From now on, I will embrace my tired eyes. They will appear seemingly dead, impossible to read. My secrets will remain buried. You will like me better this way. This entire coast has tired eyes; I am certain of it. James De Valle drives fast automobiles and Donald Humphrey shakes politicians' hands. They both wave and smile, their eyes tired as hell. The street bum pressed against the side of Peterson's Liquor, throwing his last dollar down on a game of cee-lo, has tired eyes, too. Charlie has the most tired eyes of them all. Hell, we were all as tired as old Charlie, each of us plugging into different outlets, trying to comprehend how tired we actually could become.

Signed,
J.B.

I closed my journal while the van drifted through the last tree-shaded bend. Sunlight washed across my body as Eli used the wipers to clear away the pine needles that had collected like snow on the windshield. Mary Ann Lewis sat beside me looking out the side window as the ocean became visible again. Her eyes had dried. I gathered the flower petals still pressed against my corduroy slacks. I placed my hand outside the van and watched as each petal slowly slipped from my grasp. The sky was the brightest of blues. As the petals were taken with the wind, I felt no remorse. I too, was beautiful once.

CHAPTER
— 14 —

I could feel my attachment to Mary Ann Lewis growing even though we had been together for only two weeks and we had made love only once.

The night I left Doctor Henry P. Whitehouse's office for good—the night I walked under Mary Ann Lewis's red umbrella for the first time—well, that night when I returned home via taxi with King curled under my jacket and Eli passed out drunk on the couch in his Admirals gear, Mary Ann was waiting for me outside the gate of my estate, soaking wet. Pun. Just kidding about the pun, I was not that cool.

She had no explanation for her appearance at my home, and I would never ask for one. Inside, I lit a fire and carried Eli up into his room in the East Hall. I changed into my old red-and-blue sweater and poured two glasses of a 1995 Pinot Noir Doris had stored in the wine cabinet. I returned to the living room to find Mary Ann sitting completely naked in front of the fire, her small breasts exposed and seemingly flickering at the mercy of the burning logs. Closing my eyes, I can still hear the logs breaking and bending much like the spines of two lovers entwined.

As my attachment to Mary Ann Lewis grew, I hated myself for it. Her love made me feel weak. I understood that this is what I had wanted—to steal her away and taste everything in a spirited free fall; however, I had arrived at an unforeseen catch: the mushrooms had led me to perceive the pressing weight of a new relationship. Yes, I had a reason to be better; however, I also had expectations to fulfill—expectations I wasn't sure I could keep. My feeling of well-being had become dependent on Mary Ann Lewis loving me and me loving her.

Earlier in the day, before we ate mushrooms, we stopped for breakfast. Mary Ann Lewis had to take a call outside, so I gave her a quarter to feed the pay phone along the side of the diner. I guess the cell reception was poor. I went inside the restaurant hoping to take a piss, but the bathroom was out of order, so I exited out the diner's backdoor and relieved myself behind a tree. About a half-mile inland, the air was warm and birds were singing merrily in the pines above me as I finished up my business. I felt my stomach growl, and I was about to go back inside when I heard Marry Ann Lewis's voice along the side of the building. I couldn't help but listen even though I knew I shouldn't. I overheard her tell the person on the other end of the receiver that she "really liked me."

From that moment on I felt an extreme amount of pressure to remain likeable. Everything was safer when Mary Ann Lewis was out of reach and unattainable. I realized, as she rested her head on my shoulder, that she was no longer just something great for me to contemplate while walking the thirty-six steps from the elevator landing to the Doctor's office. At that moment when I overheard her on the phone, she had become something great for me to eventually lose.

It had become apparent that I needed her, just like I needed Buddhism, and just like I needed the pills. I felt uncomfortable putting her love inside of me in an effort to make myself feel better. I couldn't use her in that way; I was happy, and it felt wrong. I was a walking contradiction, whereas I wanted to be as simple as flower petals in the wind.

As I contemplated a free-falling existence, the setting Sun and the consistent hum of the old VW engine helped me organize my thoughts. I knew then what I had to do. I reached into my pack and pulled out a bottle of wine and some crackers. Swigging straight from the bottle, I passed the crackers around the car and everyone seemed to be more than fine. I fed a few crackers to King and even let him lick some wine from the palm of my hand. I pulled my journal from my pack and started to write again:

> ...*pulling outside the pines the setting Sun cast few shadows in its descent. The Sun is the most tired of all the*

planets in the solar system, caring for all the others with love. On Earth, the Sun is married to the West, and in California the Sun faithfully returns to the Pacific every night. This ritual must be out of love. And as the various lengths of light are pushed across the reflective ocean surface, I can't help but notice they all seemed to lead to the planet Me. A planet that seemed uninhabitable at times. As Eli's foot fell harder against the accelerator, we were pulled faster and faster. However, the light still led to me. I found comfort in knowing that the light would always lead to me. I found comfort in knowing that some things had an infinite home...

I could feel my world slow as I put my journal away for the day. The writing and deep thought had made me carsick. My eyes were heavy, but my mind kept spinning strange patterns. Every time I closed my eyes, I saw kaleidoscope maps, and my body felt warmer than ever with Mary Ann resting her head across my shoulder and King resting in my lap. I wanted to sleep but something loomed deep within me that I knew I couldn't avoid. I had *ten* pills left and the rapture would come, I was sure of it. I would need to be alone for it. I would need to leave Mary Ann and King and my brother before I got nasty, before I became unlikeable.

There was only about an hour left until we reached San Luis Obispo, where we had planned on spending the night on the beach beneath the stars, just like we had the previous summer up in Oregon. I slowly guided

Mary Ann Lewis off my shoulder with a hand on her back, and I laid her to rest against the van window.

The Sun had set and moonlight reflected off the ocean, making Mary Ann Lewis's skin look pale, painting her blonde hair silver. She was beautiful, but I couldn't love her through a broken mind. I couldn't imagine what twisted things I would do in my sickness to sabotage our new relationship.

Hell, I was feeling nasty already just thinking about it.

I lifted King up with a hand under his belly. He had grown but was still a puppy nonetheless, small enough to sleep on my lap. I set the Dalmatian atop Mary Ann Lewis's legs, which were up on the seat, crossed like applesauce, her head pressed against the window in a deep sleep.

I could tell Eli was tired, too, so I asked to take the wheel. We pulled over to the side of the road, where he slid into the passenger's seat and I pushed open the side door adjacent to King and Mary Ann. The cold night air kissed my face and pushed itself throughout my body, causing my spine to straighten like the tightening of a child's jump rope. The light from inside the van splashed out on the pavement, which was cool on my bare feet. Eli was already fast asleep in the passenger's seat, his mesh hat that read *Mitch's Surf Shop* pulled down over his face. I reached inside the van and grabbed my backpack, sliding another bottle of wine into its fold. I closed the side door as softly as I could, saying these words to King before the door light went dark, "Be good."

I crept around the side of the van, my eyes bulging like two full moons, a finger running along the grain of the wood panel. Mary Ann Lewis's face was pressed against the window, her light, womanly breathing fogging the glass. I stood there for five minutes or so just watching her sleep. Watching her sleep, watching her breath kiss the window like the tide kisses a shoreline. I remembered that night how we lay curled by the fireplace, the cracking and the bending of the logs, the pitter-patter of the rain falling on the ceiling, our bodies twisting in and out. I could feel her breath then, like I could see it at that moment in the window. I stood in that memory until I couldn't hold it any longer, and eventually my own reflection appeared in the glass like an emerging ghost. I looked tired and scared, but mainly tired. Large purple circles had formed beneath my eyes. I stood watching her sleep. I could have whispered something along the lines of "I'm sorry," though I didn't. I probably should have said I was sorry.

CHAPTER
— 15 —

Barefoot on Highway 101, I was able to hitch a ride from a lonely trucker named Clay Thomas. He was a fat man, bearded and skeptical, who loved to talk and chew tobacco, oftentimes spitting down the front side of his blue-jean shirt that was embroidered "Cla," the letter *y* having come unraveled.

It was all rather entertaining, and I liked listening to the man talk. He had a myriad of conspiracy stories, and he didn't mind if I drank wine and put my dirty feet up on the dash. I offered him some wine as well, but he was a recovering alcoholic.

"Tha's why I chew so much," he said and let out a bellowing laugh, spewing a large amount of brown spit into a gigantic Jack in the Box cup.

The most compelling conspiracy theory he had was about the social networking site Facebook. I wasn't sure what use a fifty-year-old trucker for Waxie Sanitary Supply had with Facebook. He couldn't have had more than two or three close friends in his life, probably truckers, too, who were always on the road. Nor was I sure what use came from his beef with the social network. Nonetheless, Clay Thomas had cooked up an idea that was attempting to poison my exploding mind.

His theory was simple: Facebook was a tool created by the United States government and fronted by federal agent Mark Zuckerberg with the purpose of spying on citizens throughout America. First developed as a means of discovering market trends by studying the personal information U.S. citizens shared on the site. The government's first authorized super-cookie.

Information assumed by the public to be confidential was then compiled and used with the purpose of rebuilding the economy in George Bush's first term as president "after the giant birds crashed into the buildings."

However, the American people proved to be a mess in their psychology. The government quickly learned how vain society had become; almost all of the content was irrationally self-involved and proved useless in predicting economic or market trends.

Bush thought about scrapping the program entirely. However, based on a recommendation from his father, also named George Bush, who was also president at a much earlier time, the younger Bush moved the Facebook program from the economics department to the much larger defense department.

The U.S. Defense Department had a huge budget and could afford to advance the software of the program so that it could creep throughout all the devices on which one's Facebook profile was accessed, primarily computers and mobile devices. Like a stealthy spider, it would crawl through webs of personal information, email accounts, call history, bank accounts, calendars, you name it, searching for anything "threatenin' to the Rud, White, and Blue."

"Ova five hundrud million users globally, they say that on the radio the otha' day, and I tell ya, John...," Clay Thomas kept calling me John, "...nothing is safe. It's the twenty-first century. Cops ain't out here on the road or in the cities. No, no, no minor men out on the highways and in cities to give ya speeding tickets and arrest drunken college students. Thas all nothing but a front to make the people think the government's in the *right* amount of control."

Clay Thomas turned the radio low. "The real cops, John..." He spit into his gigantic Jack in the Box cup. "The real cops are in your computer."

I understood what Clay was trying to say; however, I had no worries for America or any other country. The government could probe and probe. And I figured they'd find the same self-involved shit we've always known. Still, I couldn't help but think how far gone Clay Thomas was and how America had made him that way. The man had been all over the country inside that truck delivering Waxie goods to all its major outlets, maybe resting overnight at a Waxie warehouse in Cincinnati or Chicago. He was making a clean American living, the same way his father, Jud Thomas, had. "Ain't nothing more clean than livin' with eighteen unda'neath, John."

Clay had stretched coast to coast, and as we sat in the front seat of his truck he had a fear of computers and technology, whereas I just had distaste for those things. I liked the man; I really did. However, something told me I had to keep moving. And I got my chance just inside Los Angeles, when Clay Thomas pulled the truck off the highway to stop at a Shell gas station. I was feeling uneasy when Clay got out of the truck. He walked around the front of the cab and deposited the Waxie company credit card into the gas machine. He then disappeared toward the end of the rig and began fiddling with the pump. I pressed the seat cushions for change.

"Hey, John," Clay said, startling me. I looked down at him from the cab. "Imma gonna go get a tin," he said. "You watch the pump."

Of course I said, "Of course." And when he disappeared inside the service station—I split.

I had found a quarter lodged in the driver's seat cushion, and two blocks away, I found a pay phone where I dialed the only person I knew in Los Angeles. I had discovered his number written on a small piece of paper wedged between a Berries Frozen Yogurt card and the leather fold of my wallet.

CHAPTER
— 16 —

Outside a downtown Los Angeles bar, I bummed a cigarette from a man who looked like Jesus. The name of the bar was The Lantern. I had never been there, but the name was painted in large, faded-yellow writing against its redbrick exterior. I had walked all the way from the phone booth. The bouncer wouldn't let me in because I was still barefoot, having left my shoes in the back seat of the van where Mary Ann Lewis, Eli, and King slept silently along Highway 101.

It was fine. The stars were high, and the air was cool and nice to breathe. I was just planning on killing some time anyway while I waited for the only person I knew in Los Angeles. He was approaching through the shadows of the street, his collar pulled high like a curtain closing on his godly face. The people on the street and accompanying balconies shouted for an encore, one more holy monologue, one more glance at his handsome face.

James De Valle's eyes were shining a little less brightly than those two blue orbs I had seen at the Chrysanthemum Foundation's annual ball. Still, he studied me with interest outside the bar. The bouncer looked surprised and somewhat embarrassed that he had just stopped a friend of James De Valle's, one of "Hollywood's Hottest Actors" (according to the *LA Reporter*), from entering the bar.

"James Buffalo!" James De Valle shouted as he drew me close into a warm embrace. "You're alive. I thought you done near drank yourself to death like Jack up at Big Sur. But here you are in Los Angeles, shoeless, without a dime!"

"Well, I've got a half bottle of wine in my pack, and I'm still waiting to hear back from Jack about our Big Sur trip," I replied.

We both laughed, but it wasn't very funny. Jack really did almost drink himself to death up at Big Sur. He died years later, his body permanently shut down from alcoholism.

"Hey, I have been thinking about that *Bad Dharma* you told me about—" he started.

"It's shit." I cut him off.

I had given up on my twisted Buddhism; it was just another pill that I really never understood how to take. I couldn't take anything anymore. Love, modern drugs, and old ideas—they all seemed too tough to swallow. *Well, maybe a few drinks*, I thought, anything to keep my mind from exploding.

James De Valle took a strong drag of his cigarette. When he inhaled the smoke, he left the grit in his mouth; he always did this. I supposed it was too much effort to lift his arms for something so trivial as burning paper and dried leaves. Upon drawing a breath, the crooked cig between his slender lips would rise up like a stray weed on old sidewalk reaching for some daylight.

After a few seconds and a few more handless puffs of tobacco, James De Valle turned to the bouncer, who still had his eyes locked on the both of us, his head tilted, mouth open to the side as if he just had a few stones pulled by the dentist.

"Fucker wouldn't let me in." I motioned downward with my eyes. "No shoes." James De Valle nodded and smiled, looking down at my pale bare feet glowing against the smog-stained asphalt, like two bars of chalk soap sliding down West Avenue. Exhaling smoke with a heavy breath, he removed the cigarette from his mouth with his right hand and turned toward the bouncer. The man's face went rigid upon detection. I imagined he wished he could sink into the brick exterior of the bar undetected like a ghost at a graveyard.

James De Valle laughed, tossing the half-gone cig to the ground, warm embers splitting from its tip, spitting like fallen stars across a Christmas sky, a few of them landing on my naked toes. I squirmed and James De Valle shrugged as he extended his left hand toward the bouncer, drawing the bird.

We headed east on West Avenue, away from the bar, where a crowd had formed. Passing under the streetlights, we laughed at a paparazzo who was caught on the palm-covered median waving an arm madly in our direction, simultaneously juggling a large camera in the other. Fittingly, two yellow taxis zipped up to the curb on both sides of him, assuming he was trying to flag a ride.

"Los Angeles!" I shouted, smiling ear to ear.

"Yeah, you said it, buddy," replied James De Valle. He turned on his heels and I could see him blush. He almost seemed ashamed about the attention his presence brought. The people outside of the bar, the bouncer, the man caught on the center median— they had no idea who he really was. Yet they worshiped him, like a god. And James De Valle knew he was not a god; he knew the difference between the Bible and the *LA Reporter*. And deep down, he felt neither would accept him if they knew he was a homosexual.

Still, he was human, so naturally he loved the attention he hated. He dated the most attractive women to protect the front, trophies in every sense of the word, and drank till he was content. At the time, James De Valle assumed I did not know he was a homosexual. And he would never tell me. He was trapped, left ashamed of his talents and all his beauty. I got off on knowing things like this. James wasn't an artist; he was the art. And I could see something in this "art" that only a few had, or ever would. I could see the sadness. America had made him. America had made this piece of art, just like America had driven Clay Thomas mad, and, man, did I love it all.

I wished Doris were with me beneath the street lamps and tall buildings, breathing in the sticky smell of gasoline fumes caught up in the cold, heavy air that winter nights bring. I wished she would finish her novel and climb down back into all the happenings of life. The buzzing of the bees, if you will.

I needed her. Not like how I needed Mary Ann Lewis. I needed Doris like a wolf needs the moon. I just needed her to hear my howling. I needed her to know I wasn't well, whereas I needed Mary Ann to feel well or sad. Doris would have loved to see Los Angeles with me, all grown up and raw. All the life and all the characters roaming the streets together, she would have loved it.

"So these should fit," said James De Valle. "They're actually a little small on me, so just keep them if you like. You said you were a size ten, right?" We crossed the street to escape the crowd. "I wore these in the *Lone Ranger* remake," he explained, shoving a pair of dark leather boots into my stomach, and then motioning for a taxi.

It was my turn to blush. I wasn't sure why. I guessed that all the unwarranted kindness made me turn red.

Inside the cab I thought of vegetable fried rice as my stomach growled, and I examined the leather boots in my lap. I closed my eyes, taking in the rich smell of leather.

"Thanks, James," I replied with a heavy breath. I must have looked so tired, I thought. My eyes felt dead, but my heart was beating strong.

"Do you like?" he asked.

"More than you know," I said.

"Yeah?" he said.

"Yeah, and don't worry," I replied.

"Worry?" he said confused.

"Yeah, don't," I said.

"Worry about what?" he asked.

"The sweat and the blood," I said.

"What sweat, what blood?" he asked, looking the boots over.

"Exactly!" I shouted.

"James Buffalo, you're a strange dude," he said with a smile.

"I know. Say, you know any Chinese food places around here? I'm starving." And I was.

James De Valle knew of a "damn good Chinaman restaurant," but he didn't want to eat there because ever since he starred in a foreign action film alongside Casey Wong he was "pretty big amongst the Asians as well." I agreed that we should eat unencumbered, and he had the taxi take us back to his suite at the Grand Marriott in downtown Los Angeles.

"You live in a hotel?" I asked, pressing my boots firmly into the marble lobby floor. Pivoting back and forth on my heels, I pretended to reach for holsters on my hips, drawing and pointing my fingers at the cute receptionist. She was a little brunette, freckled, with large brown eyes and her hair tied up in a little bun. She giggled. And then fumbled with some papers on the reception desk. She adjusted her thin tortoise-frame glasses. I watched as her cheeks flushed rosy red like a young child's cheeks turn rosy red after playing in the snow.

"I live in a hotel," James De Valle repeated to himself. "Should I live in a mansion?" he asked.

I couldn't tell if he was just playing around or if he honestly wanted my opinion on his place of residence.

"No, that's where I live. I mean *lived*."

"Ha," James De Valle laughed as we entered the elevator. "Where you *lived*. That's funny, James. I'll see you at the Chrysanthemum Foundation's annual ball next year, same place, right? Big ol' mansion on the beach! Ha, you're somethin', buddy." Inside the elevator he pointed at the panel of buttons and said, "Guess which floor?"

"Twenty-seven!" I shouted.

"How'd ya know?" he said softly.

"It's the top floor," I said.

"Yeah, I know, and you don't live in a mansion—" He paused and pressed the button, almost disappointed in us both. "Say, if you don't live in that big mansion anymore, where ya live now, James Buffalo?"

"Well," I began, and then paused. As we started upward I couldn't help but think about the Buffalo Estate. I imagined the overgrown landscaping, crooked cars parked in the driveway, and Doris tucked up tight in the guest residence, burning her oil lamp and pressing the quill to paper. I thought of Eli, Mary Ann Lewis, and King sleeping in the van. I thought of myself now in the elevator, ascending to the top of a Los Angeles Marriott with James De Valle, and I said, "Where do I live?" I paused again for dramatic emphasis, letting out a nervous chuckle. "Planet Earth, of course."

"Really," said the actor, his voice a whisper. He then lowered his head so that a dark-brown curl of hair fell across his eyes and slender nose. Looking around the elevator he made sure we were alone, even though he knew we were. He then winked at me, and raised his head, "I've never been."

I surveyed the elevator to make sure we were alone, even though I knew we were. "It blows," I whispered.

"Really?" James De Valle laughed sullenly. The actor did not smile. Instead he looked down at his feet and said, "James, we're all playing parts. The twenty-seventh floor isn't really me. This isn't my home—"

"DING!" interrupted the elevator as we jolted to a stop and stepped out into the marble landing of the loft.

"My home... ," the actor said, lifting his gaze out toward the Los Angeles skyline where the hills flickered, the city's buildings all ashine and lit like lanterns. "My home is buried beneath the great Wyoming sky, somewhere on my parents' ranch. It is not here in Los Angeles, and I don't think I will ever make this my home, James."

"Why's that?" I said.

"Well, I didn't leave home when I left for Los Angeles," he said. "I left home when I first felt that desire to find something better in life. I left home the second I felt I deserved more than those Wyoming skies."

I didn't reply, though I thought I understood what he was saying. I had heard Charlie tell me the same thing numerous times outside of Peterson's Liquor when I asked him to come stay with us during the cold winter months. "I have only lived in one home in this life, James, and it is right here beneath this sky!" he'd say, stamping a foot into the ground. I couldn't help but wonder when I, too, had decided I deserved more than everything. I wished I had something to say right then to reaffirm what James De Valle was saying, but I didn't, and we just looked at each other in an awkward silence.

After a half minute or so, James De Valle perked up and slapped his palms on my shoulders. "Well, that was a load of bullshit, hey?" He threw his elevator card on the steel and glass table. "Ha," he laughed. "I crack myself up sometimes. I swear I can't turn this shit off. That was almost straight out of *The Lone Ranger*."

I could tell he didn't mean it. And I could tell he felt as though he had revealed too much of himself. So, like a man, I pretended I couldn't see his hurt, and I would do my best to hide my own in return.

The actor then crossed the room and slid open the glass doors to his balcony, which instantly lit up with dim blue mood lighting, and he motioned for me to follow. Once we were outside, he pulled two cigars from his jacket pocket and with an arm around my shoulder and the dancing hills of Los Angeles glowing in the distance, he gave me a good shake and said, "The twenty-seventh floor has only one flat, James Buffalo, and let's say we fill it with people."

CHAPTER
— **16** —
and a Half

We never ordered Chinese food, and it was fine because that night we were going to fill up on the cancer that is Los Angeles. I had to call down to the lobby to invite the cute receptionist with freckles up to James De Valle's suite on the twenty-seventh floor. It wasn't a hard sell. The receptionist, whose name was Frances French, agreed to bring up some candy bars and potato chips from the lobby snack room. I was delighted. I too was turning rosy red.

James De Valle had filled his apartment with contemporary art and uncomfortable furniture. I sat almost horizontal on a hard leather armchair, studying the painting of a man kissing a dog, which was hanging awkwardly above the sweeping glass-fronted fireplace. I mean, this guy was really *kissing* a dog—his tongue was interlocked with the German shepherd's like a twisted pretzel. It would have been really sick. However, the whole thing seemed to reek of an irony that couldn't be taken seriously.

I asked James De Valle what his favorite piece of art was. He pointed, nonchalantly sipping bourbon from a small crystal glass, and said, "The Victorian over there." I pried my body from the sticky newness of the leather chair. I stood up and started to drift across the room, taking in everything through my tired eyes, my boots clicking, my compass turned west.

Despite its unfriendly navigation, I liked James's place, the only suite on the twenty-seventh floor. It was the top of the castle, the castle where the city kept its king safe, safe from the dirt-stained serfs who walked the streets smoking cigarettes in dirt-stained T-shirts that maybe read, "Nirvana" or "Los Doyers." I liked the way my leather boots clicked on the granite floors in the living room, lobby, and bedroom. I liked the way I could see my own faint reflection like a ghost in the bay windows while simultaneously surveying all of downtown Los Angeles. There were so many lights.

In the corner of the room, I found the Victorian he referred to, a marble statue of a naked man who happened to have a rather large dangle.

Yeah, I bet this is your favorite *piece*, I thought to myself.

I felt trite and cheap at my own coldness to my host's sexual orientation, my brain's manual clicking of a small-time comedy, stewing as a result of some nervousness I did not fully understand.

It's just good ol'-fashioned American programming, I thought. The same programming the rest of the sphere was spinning, or was it something greater than social conditioning? That train of thought led me to the mother lode of all theories, a theory bigger than Clay Thomas's Facebook debacle, the theory that some great Architect programmed people from birth. I wasn't sure how I felt about this, though sometimes I really wished it were true. If I were programmed beyond my control, it would put to rest all the nasty and shameful thoughts that crept into my head. *Not my fault*, I could tell myself, *I was programmed a fool*.

Still, could it ever be that simple? I mean, why try to even rationalize thought if everything was beyond your control? Where's the sauce, where's the gasoline? I was burning gasoline. I was fueled with life, and the sadness only made me want more. And the inheritance I knew I had waiting for me (if I chose to play along) made me feel slow and dirty, whereas I needed to feel fast and alive. Society had told me to eat the grapes of wealth and find happiness in its juices. Is that the Bible blueprint, to be fat and happy, to conquer social ladders? No, the fat and happy part was definitely American programming. Yeah, I was sure of that.

James De Valle's suite had a view of Staples Center, which was letting out a Kings hockey game at the moment, the crowd flowing out like ants from an anthill, while my brain continued to click. The manual clicking of nervousness never stopped for me. I needed a pill; I needed to move my mouth; I needed to laugh at what I should; I needed to say what I was programmed to say;

I needed to react how I should; I needed to scream to the people below that James De Valle was a fag!

These thoughts made me want to crush my ghost-like figure in the glass, but I knew I couldn't, and I knew I never would. And I didn't believe in a great Architect either. So I stood there on the twenty-seventh floor of a downtown Los Angeles Grand Marriott, watching as every last person exited Staples Center, trying to love it all.

CHAPTER
— 17 —

Twenty minutes passed and there was still no sign of Frances French, the cute receptionist. I was beginning to get antsy again. I really needed my pills. I tried to read *The Way to Freedom*, which was stuffed in my backpack's center pocket from months ago. I couldn't understand any of the Dalai Lama's teachings, even the parts I had underlined, and, seriously, I just wanted another pill. I hadn't taken any since I was last on the bus some eight hours before, and my drunk was starting to plateau, leaving me about as stable as a Japanese Ping-Pong ball.

In the guest room, I saw that James De Valle had laid out a shirt and some dark blue jeans for me to change into, since my threads were obviously too dirty for the top of the castle. I took a shower, washed, and watched the dirt from my feet spiral down the drain. I thought I would finally have another pill, so I finished my shower and loosely combed my hair using my hands in the steam-kissed mirror. I wrapped a towel around my waist and stepped out of the bathroom. I surveyed the room. I couldn't find my pack anywhere, and it had my prescription bottle in it. I could have sworn I had left it at the foot of the guest bed. I noticed *The Way to Freedom* was still on the bed, spine open from before. My journal was closed next to it. I hadn't remembered taking it out; maybe I had. My pack was nowhere to be found. I slid into the blue jeans James had left for me. I assumed they were his. I had to roll the ankles up a good three to four times to prevent them from dragging on the floor. I pulled on my boots and picked up the shirt James De Valle had given me. It was a nice shirt, a black button-down that fit me well, and I was pleased enough. The shirt was expensive. I could tell because it had a small blue crocodile above the right breast pocket. Crocodiles are expensive, especially blue ones. If you remember, Charles David Buffalo had claimed to kill a crocodile for his boots. If you remember, Charles David Buffalo was full of shit.

James said a friend had left the shirt, though I'm sure it was probably one of his lover's shirts. It definitely wasn't Donald M. Humphrey's. There was no way he could fit into it. I imagined him trying to and laughed loudly to myself—I did not feel guilty.

James De Valle was still getting dressed in his bedroom, which was shyly lit by candlelight, the candles putting off a soft vanilla smell that drifted through the guest bedroom. I continued to search for my pack. In time I gave up as the aroma of vanilla led me to the master bedroom, where the walls were high and perfectly white, glowing at the mercy and sporadic flickering of the candles. The windows were draped by opposing waves of maroon curtains, a small sliver of moonlight entering at the center where the two sleeves kissed. I followed the beam of escaping moonlight all the way to my boots as I stood in the doorway.

I took a step forward and turned my gaze upward to observe a large painting of a beachside cottage. The painting was hanging at the heart of the room above two spiral wooden bedposts, on a wall adjacent to a seventy-inch television. The television, a Sony, was not plugged in, and it never had been. I could tell because I was standing right next to it, and the pronged, coiled electrical cord extending from the rear of the television was caked with a thick layer of dust.

The painting depicted what was most likely a cottage on the Carolina Coast. I was sure of that, although I had never been. The cottage was fashioned with white wooded shingles, shingles made soft by the salt of the ocean, the artist wanted you to think. In reality, they were made soft by the artist's calm brush strokes and the calculated mixing of paints, most likely white, blue, and grey. The artist's brain had clicked manually, like mine, like yours, and I couldn't blame him for leading me to believe his art was anything more than paint.

"James, does this place exist? Have you been?" I asked, stepping up onto the tightly made king-sized bed to further examine the painting. The gold satin comforter barely flinched beneath my leather boots. I wanted to run my fingers along the slate-colored sea grass that sprouted along the dirt road leading up to the cottage. And I wanted to bury my feet deep in the brown sand on the beach, like two spoons dipping into peanut butter ice cream.

"Does what exist?" he mumbled.

"The cottage, in the painting," I replied with a laugh, running a hand through my hair, which still felt dirty, even though I had just taken a shower. My hair was growing long again, and I had to pull it back to keep the dark curls off my forehead and out of sight. Dirty hair is good for this because it listens and goes where it should. Clean hair never listens. Eli always ran a hand through his hair when he was talking, and at that moment I pictured him doing it, his hair longer and dirtier than mine. I missed Eli. I felt bad for leaving him along Highway 101. Soon enough, he would wake up and find the note I had left inside of his cigarette pack. He would run a hand through his dirty hair, which would listen, and he would read:

Eli,

I think they were right when they said I wasn't well. Tell Mary Ann Lewis, I am sorry.

James

I looked again at the painting. Doris had taken Eli and me to a cottage in the Midwest once; it was nice. I could have only been nine or ten years old at the time, in my "prime exploring stage of childhood development," according to *The Raising of Eli and James Buffalo: America's Reveling Youth.* I loved Doris, but I really hated that book. It was too personal and too smart.

Anyway, Doris took us to visit an old college friend whom she used to protest with at Berkeley. The cottage was on Lake Michigan and it was old and beautiful. So was the beach; well, they call it "the beach" in the Midwest, but really it's not. Anyone who has ever been West would tell you it is not the "the beach." Still, if they were decent and good they would tell you it was nice, which it was.

I remember the sand the most. It's different from the sand in the West; it's heavy and coarse. My favorite part was digging deep into that heavy sand up away from the shoreline where the tall green grass that led down from the foot of the cottage's wooden stairs started to thin. It was just outside where the grass thinned that I would dig some hundred yards away from the calm vastness of Lake Michigan. It was there where the grass thinned that I would reach deep into cold heavy sand, mining for toads. With my eyes closed and hands buried, I would wait until I could feel the cold rippled skin and faint heartbeat of the sleeping amphibian, and with a jerk I would up and take off, away from where the grass thinned, past the rusty bicycle at the foot of the wooden stairs. And with my hands behind my back, I would eventually reveal to Doris my prize. So, with my boots pressing into the gold satin covers, I asked James De Valle once again, louder this time, if the cottage existed.

"Ha," laughed the actor as he examined himself in his bathroom mirror.

"Well, does it?" I said even louder.

"Well, yes, it does," he said uninterested.

"Can I go?" I said.

"Go where?" James De Valle backtracked as he examined his hands before dipping them into the sink. The counter top was the color of salmon flesh, and I watched water begin to trickle off the pink ledge and down to the dark granite flooring.

"The cottage, in the painting," I said again.

"Huh," he mumbled.

"Are you—," I said starting to get angry.

"I can't feel my face," James De Valle interrupted as he removed his cupped hands from the sink, cautiously lifting the water to his face as though he were lifting baby Jesus from the hay.

"What?" I shouted.

"I can't feel my face. Hold on," he said. He splashed the water in his hands against his face. "No, nothing."

I stepped across the room and into the bathroom, where the actor stood in his briefs, and turned the faucet shut. "Are you okay?" I asked.

"James, I took your pills. I am sorry, but I did," he said with a twinge of concern. Concern for his well-being, of course; he had no idea what he had just done to me. Actors can be selfish like this. I knew exactly what he was going to say.

"The pain-killers, the pills in your pack. I took them." He pointed back toward the foot of the master bed. Below the painting of the cottage, I saw my backpack sitting there inconspicuously in the dim candlelight like it should, its centerfold open and gaping as if to tell me it had just been gutted. My dirty clothes had been tossed aside, and I saw my pill bottle, barren on the granite floor. I was left with a steady lack of breathing and overall silence of raw confusion.

"I can replace them tenfold. I was planning on it. Trust me, James! I just wanted to start early, you know?" I heard the actor say.

"Those weren't pain-killers," I croaked, staring at my pack as it gaped wide-open back at me.

"Are you serious? They looked like Vicoden, or Oxy. And I saw you take the pills from Anna at the Chrysanthemum Ball, and I thought I could, *you know*, start early..." His voice began to drift off until it was nothing more than an audible hissing sound, like hot air escaping from a balloon.

I watched as my pack began to grow in size, its metal zipper teeth unraveling at the sides, its mouth growing and growing at the corners. I watched as it opened wider and wider, showing me its hollow insides, the pit of its gutted stomach.

Before I knew it, I was moving.

I walked clean across the room, passing my gutted pack, passing the unplugged Sony. I followed the thin strip of moonlight on the floor to the window. I felt the soft fabric of the curtains. "These are nice!" I shouted. "They must be foreign!" I then leaned backward toward the master bed with twin fists grasping the respective curtain sleeves. I laughed as gold metal rivets along the ceiling began to pop. Like a thief rappelling down a building, I hung from the curtains, collecting bits of white stucco on my hair and my shoulders as the rivets began to give way. I got a rush when I collapsed backward onto the bed. The metal railing that was holding the curtains broke free as the last rivet gave way. The metal rod had split in two, and the smaller piece, which was only about three feet long, struck me across the lower lip.

I lay on my back, laughing as the silver moonlight bathed my body and the slow trickle of blood ran down my chin onto the expensive shirt, the one with a blue crocodile stitched above the right breast pocket.

Turning my face and wiping away the blood on my face with my forearm, I noticed one of the curtains had landed on a candle and started to burn. The flames were small and eventually they dwindled and died.

"THOSE WEREN'T PAIN-KILLERS!" I shouted. I picked up the metal rod that had struck me, and I started back toward the crumpled actor.

"Whatever they are, chmmm, were…" I could hear him talking, "I was going to replace them tenfold. I have a guy coming tonight."

"How much did you take?" I said pointing the rod in his direction.

"All of them," he replied and trembled.

"All of them?" I smiled.

"Fuck, do I even want to kn—," he started.

"They are high-dose antidepressants. I needed those," I told him.

"Why do you need antidepressants?" he asked.

"Well, James, it doesn't really fucking matter to you," I yelled.

"I am sorry, man. I got a guy. I can replace them. Jesus, what is wrong with me? James, I'm sorry, man. What are they?" James De Valle asked again. He dropped to his knees and tears began to form in the corners of his narrowing eyes.

"There will be no replacing," I said, my voice raspy. I glanced in the mirror, seeing my hair powdered stucco white and my lip bleeding. I felt little mercy, though I should have. I couldn't. I was growing, beyond the manual clicking. I was cold changing. My atmosphere had been strung high and tight. I had no more pills. My mind had no schedule. I was wide open. Yeah.

I felt the coldness of the metal rod in my hand, and I watched as James De Valle's tears turned into scales and fell to the granite floor in sick piles, which I kicked to the side. I began to laugh hysterically.

I thought about putting some blood on my boots. Yeah, I looked at the flesh beneath me. I could have. He was a snake, after all. And I easily could have snapped my boots down on the back of the serpent's neck, protecting myself from its poisonous fangs, watching as it up and turned, eventually wrapping the skinny end of its body around my ankle until it did nothing but twitch and twitch, like I used to *click* and *click*, life coming and going. It all seemed pretty strange and beautiful to me.

CHAPTER
— 18 —

I slammed James De Valle's bedroom door in a panic. I looked at my hands as they started to shake. *I have to get out of this fucking Marriott*, I thought. I could already hear voices coming from the living room. It appeared the party was under way. Earlier in the night I had noticed a fire escape outside of a window at the hallway's dead end. I turned outside of the doorway and crept down the adjacent hall, eyeing my escape. I heard the elevator doors open, "DING." A few people shouted as more guests arrived.

"Where's James?" I heard one partygoer ask. "Oh, you know actors; they love to make an impression," another replied. I started to run as the two burst into laughter—if only they knew.

I hit my stride halfway down the hallway. Then I heard the sound of a toilet flush and froze. I pressed against the wall as a sliver of light edged into the dark hallway. The bathroom door opened with a creak, eclipsing the window in which I planned to escape.

The bathroom door shut tentatively and the wedge of light receded. I could see the railing of the fire escape glimmer in the moonlight. The night was still and the hallway appeared deserted. *You're imagining things,* I thought. It was believable considering all that had transpired with De Valle. Then I saw her curvy figure outlined in the shadows of the night. "I thought that was you!" she purred. I could smell the cat's perfume as she swayed seductively in my direction.

"Do you always hide in hallways?" said Frances French.

"Hey, how's it going?" I said, my eyes nervously chasing the trim of her tight red dress.

"Oh, well, better now that I am off work. Say, this is a really nice—" she said placing a hand playfully on my chest.

"Well, here's the thing. I must warn you now, Frances," I said speaking very quickly. Still eyeing the fire escape I popped a cigarette into my mouth, my head bobbing emphatically while I inhaled deep to light it.

"Oh, I... ," Frances French started to speak. I motioned for her silence.

"Well, you see I am, and James is, well, not feeling, uh, well. We're both dangerous, and you seem so sweet and all in your...," I exhaled a massive puff of smoke, "...pretty red dress, you see."

"Huh?" Her mouth dropped open. "Should I call for someone?"

Seeing the panicked look on her face, I decided to pump the brakes for a second. I didn't want her to call anyone. "No, we're fine," I said and laughed nervously, running a hand through my dirty hair. "I just wanted to say you looked um, nice."

Frances French just kind of stood there, sizing me up. I hadn't actually realized how attractive she was until that moment. It was making me act weird. It occurred to me that she was more than "cute." She had changed out of that god-awful Marriott polo and into a dress that hugged her generous body like a fast car, and the way she chewed her lip let me know she was up for a chase. While she was behind the reception desk I could not tell that she was, in fact, a *woman*.

So I laughed off my naïveté and revved my engine. "What I really needed to ask you is, have you been to the Carolina Coast? It really is lovely—"

"James, did you say you weren't feeling well, or is James De Valle not feeling well? You are confusing me."

Frances French really was something to see; however, her concern upset me in the strangest of ways. "Hmmm." I leaned up against the hallway wall and smiled with a nod. I ignored her questioning and took a drag from my cigarette, upset she had interrupted me. "Having just met you, I must ask you a personal question, is that alright?" I said.

"Ah, I guess. Are you high?" she asked.

"Do you care?" I snapped.

"No, I don't think so," she said, not sure of what was going on.

"Well, I'm actually quite low. Can I ask you that question?" I pressed.

"Yes," she said after a second of silence.

"Do you read? Say yes." I thought for a second. "Mmm, 'Say Yes,' that is a great Elliot Smith song. Do you like Elliot Smith, Frances French? Say yes."

"Yes?" she said, taken aback by my shifting.

"Yes to what?" I replied.

"Well, yes, as a matter of fact, to both!" she said. "I think. But please, what is the matter with James De Valle? Is he okay? Should I phone someone? Does he have a personal doctor on hand?"

"Oh, he doesn't need any medication." I said and laughed momentarily before straightening my face and pressing my back flat against the hallway wall. "The thing is, I never said anything about De Valle."

"Well, are you okay? Your lip is bleeding. Should I get you a towel?" She reached for my face, and I respectfully turned her hand away.

"Do you read, Frances? Answer the question," I said. "Then we can talk about James."

"Is that why you are upset?" she replied.

"Well, at this very moment, no," I said with some crookedness.

"Then why are you upset?" she asked.

"I am upset because I cannot find it," I said, digging through my back pocket, looking for my flask.

"Uh, find what?" she giggled. I could tell I was growing on her.

"Found it!" I yelled.

"Uhhhhhhh, James, let me look at this cut of yours. Doesn't it burn when you drink whatever it is you're drinking?" she said and once again reached for my face, and I once again turned her hand away. I could tell she was getting irritated because her freckled nose began to scrunch and her large brown eyes began to shrink and focus on me with concern. The bad chemistry Frances French and I had was starting to show, and I felt bad for being, well, whatever it was I was being. The bad chemistry I felt made her want me more, so I played with her because I was sick and twisted, already missing Mary Ann Lewis.

"Wait, wait, wait, Frances, you never told me what was the last book you read. Please, I must know. You seem so, uh, *interesting*." I did it again. I laughed. It was the bad chemicals in me.

"Well, if you must know, it was *New Moon*," she said proudly.

"Yes, the moon is beautiful and new," I said looking out the window, "but what book, my dear? Come on, I have things to move to as well. Spit it out."

"No! You know, the Twilight books!" She laughed, sincerely nervous. "The one with Robert Patterson." Her big brown eyes begged for my approval.

"Patterson, Patterson, the author?" She reached for my face, holding a napkin she had pulled from her purse, and this time I let her wipe the blood off my chin. I continued to mumble, "Patterson, Peterson's, Peterson's

Liquor on Fourth. Yes, Charlie mentioned a Patterson. Come on, James. Now come on, you know this..."

"He plays the vampire in the *book-movie,* you silly." She laughed and placed a hand playfully on my chest while continuing to dab the blood from my split lip and my chin. She said once again, "You're silly."

Book-movie? That doesn't make any sense, I thought, *the book-movie?* Then I replied with a lie. "Oh, I remember, yes, the movies, um, James isn't feeling well—"

"Which James?" she yelled, clearly annoyed this time, pressing the brown napkin deeper into my bleeding lip.

"As a matter of fact, both Jameses aren't feeling well," I replied. "Hold on... no, I don't remember anything written by a Patterson." And with that I straightened up real good and fell straight as a log past Frances French, wide-eyed and appalled in her tight red dress. My face caught the corner of a contemporary steel table that was positioned just underneath the window. The soapy moonlight poured through the window and smoothed over my fallen body as my face hugged the coldness of contemporary tile. The dormant fire escape went unused, and Frances French let out a terrible scream as everything around me turned to black.

CHAPTER
— 19 —

As I crawled out of an avalanche of sleep, my mind momentarily clinging and pulling from consciousness like a strip of worn Velcro, I realized I had done it again. Eventually I was pulled completely awake by the strange force that is curiosity. Curious as a cat, I could dance for hours in my mind with my eyes closed tight. I knew exactly where I was, so I kept my eyes heavy and shut for a few hours, lying on my back, completely awake and completely dark. I could chase a ball of yarn for hours in my mind until I got tangled up a little too much and wound up good and sick again. So for the moment, I closed my eyes and tried to think of warmer things, like puppy dogs and Christmas lights.

When I was done pretending to be elsewhere, I opened my eyes and saw myself as I had imagined, stark naked underneath a pressed hospital gown with tiny little bluebirds on it. I had hoped that whoever undressed me was kind and professional with my naked body.

I could feel the puke-yellow hospital lights on my exposed skin, from my shins to my throbbing face, and I could taste the dank overabundance of cleaning fluids and stale humanity. The lights were always the same, so bright yet so dim at the same time, and they always made me sweat cold ice water. The kind of nervous perspiration that accumulates behind your kneecaps and lingers through your palms like a popsicle evaporating in desert sand, leaving just the faintest presence of sticky moisture behind. I could feel it beneath the puke-yellow lights, the cold dampness behind my kneecaps, which made me squirm, and my hands were as clammy as a teenage boy inside a huff house. I felt nauseous and extremely hollow. I didn't kill James De Valle, though I could have, and very much wanted to at the time.

That strange night I stood over James De Valle, I was watching my life pop and bloom like fireworks on the Fourth of July. I had pushed my toes to the front of my kicks, and I expected a grand finale. I wanted to believe that James De Valle was the culmination of this great serpent named Suffering, whom I finally trapped, unafraid. I wanted to believe I had chased my sickness down to the bathroom floor of a downtown Los Angeles Grand Marriott.

As I peered downward, I expected to see Suffering and his hideous sadness scales. I expected to see and defeat the cause of all my troubles. American television had told me that *everything* could be defeated.

I stood waiting for this great spiritual climax, waiting to crush this horrible beast I had fathered. And all I saw were my leather boots pressing into human flesh much like my own, the scales of my Suffering nowhere to be found. All I saw was the flesh of a man who looked as familiar and sad as I did, all curled up in a ball in his suite on the twenty-seventh floor. I felt tired and ashamed.

There had never been any great chase like I had hoped; there had never been any heavy fog for me to clear; and this is what had crushed me the most. All I had really been fighting was myself, James Buffalo, and, man, he was kicking some serious ass. The only thing resembling a snake I could find was the hospital's IV. It was plastic and hollow, streaming from my right forearm, a singular metal fang wedged into my bluest vein. I had put it there when I chased that ball of yarn a little too far.

I thought to myself about the bad chemistry Frances French and I had. It was ironic that I had seen her outside of James De Valle's room moments after my failed spiritual climax.

I could not help but think of how I had left Mary Ann Lewis. Eli would understand. He would understand a man's desire to flee, or more specifically a Buffalo's desire to flee. He had done it many times before, just like our father, Charles David Buffalo. I had left a letter inside Eli's cigarette pack, where I had left nothing for Mary Ann Lewis. Who knows, maybe my fleeing would make her want me more. This logic was weak, though, and I knew it. Mary Ann was too smart and free-spirited to be typecast in that way. She was no Frances French, and she was far too pretty to be lonely for long. Yeah, someday someone would shake his head and laugh when I told this sad love story. I truly was caught in a fit of *Bad Dharma*.

Eli ran away from home once when we were still sharing a room in the study's tree house. Unlike Charles David Buffalo, our father, Eli came back after about eight days of doing God-knows-what. He was only fourteen at the time, and the two of us were about to outgrow the wooden twin beds in which we slept, our feet pressing against the wooden frames whenever we lay flat on our backs. We probably should have moved out of the tree house and the tiny twin beds a few years earlier. However, we were the lost boys and we wanted to be together. When Eli left that night, he slid a note into the palm of my hand while I slept; it went something like this:

James,

I am going on an adventure just like Pan! I am going to see those little mermaids that sing to him in the cave. I will tell the lost boys you will be joining us soon! No need to worry about me, I've got all the happy thoughts in the world!

Your brother,
Eli

Eli never told anyone why he left or where he went, and it is still a mystery as to what exactly he did for those seven nights that I spent alone in the tree house. The day Eli came home was the same day I moved out of the study and up to the East Wing of the estate. This was no coincidence.

I had suspected the hospital staff had already notified Eli of my presence at whatever hospital I was in, and I would understand if he didn't come. He was probably pretty sick of me.

By then, Eli had probably arrived in San Francisco, looking to patch things up with Lucia. I was pulling for him. I really was. I wanted the phone to ring, and I wanted the little staff nurse to run into my room and tell me that I had a wedding to attend, so I'd better straighten up and comb my hair! I would tear the IV out of my forearm, and the little Hispanic nurse would notice that I was already dressed and ready to go. These were gravy dreams.

King would take me back, too. I mean, I did save him from that fat lady who used to hit him with newspapers, and I think we had some pretty good times together. Yeah, that little spotted bastard was probably missing me pretty good right about now.

Mary Ann Lewis, on the other hand, probably wouldn't be as forgiving as Eli, nor would she be as loyal as King. It was not a nice thing to do, to leave someone sleeping in a van on the side of Highway 101. It is never nice to leave someone in the middle of the night without saying good-bye or leaving a note. I knew she would probably never want to see me again, and that was a probable consequence.

CHAPTER
— 20 —

I spent the first part of my stay at Saint Victoria's Los Angeles Medical Hospital pretending to be asleep whenever the little Hispanic nurse came by my room. Under the impression I was asleep, the little nurse, with her curly black hair cut in an A-line bob, would close the curtain that divided the room in two, and she would read to my roommate, an old Chinese man who had it worse than me. He was plugged into a breathing machine that hummed and rattled like an old Afghan guitar.

The little nurse would kneel down on the floor next to the old man and pull her plain white gown slightly to the side so that it would not stretch too tight on her little body. I could hear her voice like a desert wind drifting just slightly above the rattle of the breathing machine. I wanted to hear her more. No matter how hard I pressed my ears, her voice still came through as soft, inaudible static. All I could make out was the machinery humming and the old man's occasional soft murmuring.

One day, late in the afternoon, when the sky got red and cast a pink hue across the linoleum floor, my routine got lazy and the little nurse noticed my eyes, opened and locked with the old man's. He was lying in his hospital bed with a queer smile on his face, like a Santa Barbara hipster who lies in the Santa Barbara sand, his breathing machine sounding off like an old busted radio, playing nothing but static. The old man had not a care in the world, whereas I had all the cares in the world. The old man knew this, and he sized me up real quick with his almond eyes dropped low and a hand moving across his chin, gently stroking the thin gray-black goatee that hung off his face like dead grass hangs off the side of a mountain. I was too intrigued to pretend to be elsewhere, out spinning dreams. So, when the little nurse finished reading and closed the tiny book across her plain white dress, her eyes lifted up, and mine shifted shut a little too late.

Slowly she got up, placing a hand on the old man's, and just stood there for a minute, her back to me, her hand lying on top of his. The old man's smile had faded from his face, and I could tell he was sorry she had stopped reading. The little nurse ducked low and whispered something into his ear before pulling the curtain shut, splitting the room back in two.

The little nurse did not say a word to me after she closed the curtain. And I did not know what to say, either; I was not *clicking* right, so I just lay there as she took a few notes and removed the IV from my arm. When the IV was out, she got up and left the room, her dark hair bobbing up and down. She returned a few minutes later with a *white-coat* named Dr. Weston K. Flank.

Dr. Weston K. Flank looked about my age-*ish*, realistically probably three or four years older than me, yet in time *actually lived*, I would have to say, about five or six years *less lived*. I am aware no one measures life in years *actually lived*. However, it seemed appropriate in this case. I mean, I had been racking up some serious mileage lately, whereas Dr. Weston K. Flank looked as pale and timid as a snow rabbit. To me, he was just another clean-shaven college ace whose father probably called him "Champ."

He was neither an unattractive man nor an overly attractive man. Weston K. Flank was tall, yes, and his hair was perfectly blond, yes. However, his complexion was ghost-like in his cheeks and flush red around his eyes. It was strange. Yes, very strange. He reminded me of a six-foot-tall albino koala.

"Okay, let's see, let's see, Mr. Buffalo, you're probably wondering what is wrong with you," he started in, his head tilted downward and his rather large nose protruding over his clipboard. "A-a-a-apparently so am I, hold on."

Chuckling nervously, his face turned bright red (primarily around his eyes), and he quickly exited the room and returned minutes later with a different clipboard, behind which he promptly buried his face.

"Hey. Wes," I broke my silence, but I still wasn't *clicking* right. "Do you have my cigarettes? I could really use a smoke, buddy." His awkwardness and red eyes were sparking my bad chemicals.

"You shouldn't smoke, Mr. Buffalo," he replied in cliché without lifting his koala head from behind the clipboard.

"I'm just messing with you, *Wa-a-es*," I said in a more serious tone. I imagined this made the muscles in his jaw twitch.

"I assume any belongings you had were taken when you checked in," he said, running one of his pointy fingers in a repeating east-to-west pattern across the clear-blue clipboard. "I wasn't here when they brought you in, Mr. Buffalo. However, the report indicates that you were *highly* intoxicated and suffering from a severe anti-depressant withdrawal. You shouldn't really mix the two... and you can't just stop taking a heavy dosage of antidepressants. You have to reduce your dosage gradually. Anyone can tell you that."

"I know. My plan of withdrawal was, uh, accelerated," I coughed, thinking of my gutted backpack in James De Valle's suite on the twenty-seventh floor of a downtown Los Angeles Grand Marriott.

"Well, it looks like they treated you for a minor cut across your lower lip and chin. Yes, let's see here, a girl named French, mmhhhmm, Frances French, said in the report that you fell into the corner of a steel table."

I nodded.

"Okay," he said, slightly lowering his clipboard barricade. "They attached you to an IV filled with incrementally decreasing amounts of the drug MRX2857 mixed with saline to combat the severe dehydration your body suffers during massive alcohol consumption. You understand?"

"Yes." I said meekly.

"Good. All of this was done under the consent of your brother; we phoned him. He is in San Francisco." He paused for a second to examine the rest of the report, marking down some additional notes with a ballpoint pen before lifting his head and looking at me straight with his chlorine eyes. "How are you feeling, Mr. Buffalo?"

I had to think for a second. No, nothing. I wasn't *clicking* right, so I just told him the deep down utter truth of it all. "Wes, I'm really tired."

CHAPTER
— 21 —

Dr. Weston K. Flank smiled briefly and buried his head back behind his clipboard before reemerging in all his awkward koala glory. "You shouldn't really be tired," he said. "You've been out for the last seventy-two hours."

I don't think Wes fully understood what I meant by *tired*. Too much sleep, too little sleep—it did not matter. I was sure to be tired as hell when I awoke. I couldn't stand it anymore, and I took it out on the doctor. "Are you sure you're looking at the right clipboard?" I snapped.

"Well, yes," replied Wes. He didn't blush around the eyes like I had wanted, and the muscles in his jawline didn't tighten like I expected they would. Instead, a look of concern came across his snow-rabbit face. This admittedly worried me. Wes dropped the clear-blue clipboard down to his waist. "It's not a bad thing you were out for so long, though. It makes it easier."

"Makes what easier?" I asked shortly, pulling myself into an upright position, my bare ass exposed through the back of the hospital gown.

"Sleep makes the withdrawal less painful. You're almost there. Only five more days with an IV and you'll be done with MRX2857."

"Oh, the IV." I felt the small bump on my forearm, smearing a bit of blood like finger paint. "I was wondering wha—"

"Saline and the drug MRX2857. We're weaning you off MRX2857 in incrementally smaller doses—mixed with water, of course. You can't just stop taking a drug this strong; it's too difficult on the body and the mind. I bet you feel sick, huh?" he asked, and I nodded. I did feel pretty terrible. "Much like a junkie can't just quit heroine without falling ill," Wes said. "When you are on something as strong as this, you need help. In fact, I have never seen a limbic-depressant as strong as MRX2857 prescribed for depression in citizens. Do you know the history behind this drug?" he asked.

"All I know is that it comes in a purple bottle," I told him.

"I will tell you what I know then. The drug used to be given to soldiers who had experienced extreme duress during combat in Vietnam. MRX2857 reduces the release and function of neurons in the limbic system of your brain, more specifically, the amygdala part of your brain."

"I don't know what you are saying," I interrupted.

"I am saying..." he spoke, pausing to scratch his head for a second. "I don't know why anyone would ever prescribe it to a civilian. It is very rare and hard to obtain. Not to mention illegal. We probably wouldn't have detected it in your blood. However, we have treated a lot of veterans in this hospital who have suffered nervous breakdowns after withdrawing from MRX2857, though the last veteran I treated for withdrawal from MRX2857 was back in the late seventies. It was legal in the seventies."

"The *seventies*... How old are you?"

"I just turned sixty-one last August."

"Really?"

"Never mind my age," Wes spoke more confidently, like a doctor should; he was *clicking* right. "The limbic system and the amygdala, specifically, are responsible for storing emotionally charged memories, and, simply put, MRX2857 numbs the most traumatic of these memories, distancing emotion and fact. Do you know what a limbic vice is, James?"

"Is it like a White Russian?"

I laughed to myself, wishing Eli could see all this.

Wes ignored me and pulled a burnt-orange rubber brain from one of the room's many unnoticeable beige metal cabinets. He tossed it back and forth in his hands for a second, spinning it on his index finger as if it were a basketball or an old globe. Wes then stepped closer and lowered the brain map to my level, revealing to me the hidden origins of the amygdala.

"Here!" He jabbed a bony finger into the rubber. "A limbic vice freezes movement here in the amygdala."

And I just nodded my head, like a puppy following the oversized orange tennis ball in his hands.

"MRX2857 puts the entire limbic system in a vice!" Wes shouted. The look on his face was golden as his hands squeezed the rubber brain so hard I thought it might pop; my head felt like it might do the same.

I began to feel dizzy as Wes continued. "Limbic vices are fascinating in science, still rather terrifying. The United States stopped manufacturing these types of drugs after several veterans experienced nervous breakdowns beyond repair. Luckily, Mr. Buffalo, you have not reached this state of no repair. Now, we begin the healing process!" Wes said excitedly. "In a sense, certain parts of your brain have been frozen. These frozen neurons will release as you sleep. You will have some hidden emotions that will surface soon— try to embrace them."

There was a brief moment of silence.

"My fucking brain is frozen!" I erupted in a panic, feeling nauseous. I turned over to the side of the bed as my head began to spin out of control. My vision blurred and I could barely make out a shiny bedpan that had been placed on the floor next to me. I felt my stomach muscles contract. A sharp pain shot through my lower ribs like a kicking lightning bolt. I began to viscously heave. There was nothing in my stomach except acid and plastic hospital fumes. I could dispel neither. And I could not stop the rapid compulsions that followed. The pain began to radiate through my bones. Every muscle in my body tightened, and then loosened, only to tighten harder again. I writhed in pain. Water leaked from my eyes and dripped into the hollow basin, the noise radiating like pennies bouncing around in an empty well. I repeatedly heaved toward the bedpan only to come up empty. Eventually, I felt something move in the pit of stomach, and I managed to displace about a teacup's worth of bile into the metal bedpan. A wave of relief came over me as my body loosened and began to tremble. My throat burned profusely, my eyes burned deeply as well, and my nose began to run with warm liquid.

Wes waited until I settled a bit, and he put a large hand on my shoulder. I appreciated this even though I hardly knew the man. He gave me a paper cup full of cold water, and I drank it quickly and caught my breath. I felt a lot better as the sweat on my forehead turned cold. In a few minutes, I was able to sit upright again. I watched as Wes walked to the corner of the room. He placed the burnt orange brain back into the beige cabinet from which it had come. He then turned and smiled, "Better?" he asked.

I nodded.

"Sleep helps," he said walking back to the side of my bed. He then lowered his voice a bit. "James, the hospital's psychiatrists are very skilled. They could help you cope with whatever may be troubling you."

I declined Wes's offer. I wasn't ready for anything like that. Not yet. I handed him the empty paper cup in my hand. Wes got me some more water from the sink. When he returned I thanked him. I asked him to tell me more.

"Of course," he said. "MRX2857 is still manufactured—very poorly manufactured, I might add—in the Congo and sold for very high prices on the black market. Does your doctor, Henry Whitehouse, have any connections in the Congo?"

"He may have," I croaked.

"Who?" he asked.

"My father. Though, he has passed," I said.

"I am sorry," he said and then sighed. "Do you have any idea why your father would have wanted you to get this medication?"

"I have no idea, Wes." I lied, placing the tiny paper cup to my lips. Everyone knew CDB was, to quote Hunter S. Thompson, "bat-shit-crazy."

"Well, of course you don't, James. And you may just be lying to me, and that's fine. We all know where the hurt is. When you are done here you will be able to start anew. You can very well do what you like; however, I am going to have to advise you to stay away from the drug. The danger being, without emotionally charged memories, individuals, become, well, individuals have no real context of emotion. We all have traumatic experiences, you know? The ability to have them makes us human."

I looked at Weston Flank and nodded firmly, letting him know that I did in fact understand detachment.

"Good," he said. "MRX2857 was thought to work to some extent, when one had experienced extreme duress as seen in combat, seen by some as a suitable cure for those suffering from post-traumatic stress. As we discussed, the drug targets the most extreme memories stored in the amygdala, eliminating EMR, emotional-memory-recall, by freezing the movement of the neurons surrounding the memory. In theory, a soldier prescribed MRX2857 would remember being in the war; however, they would have little memory of the war's most scarring battles. This was thought to reduce post-traumatic stress. The goal was to heal our boys emotionally so that we could deploy them again. Without these scarring memories, the soldier would harbor less anger when they thought about the war—and they would, well, they would be willing to kill again."

"Deploy them again?" I said in astonishment as my jaw dropped open.

"This was the argument, man; it was inhumane." I was beginning to see a liberal side of Wes I had not originally expected. "Why anyone would ever consent to an MRX2857 prescription on a civilian is beyond me. Though what is even more baffling is how Doctor Whitehouse obtained a steady flow of this drug, seeing that its distribution in the States was terminated by the Carter Administration in 1979 and your father has been deceased for years. It would cost a fortune to prescribe even a week's worth of MRX2857, and judging by your blood work, you have been taking this for years. You know, I am legally obligated to report this, and undoubtedly charges will be pressed against Doctor Henry Whitehouse. The United States Justice Department will crush him. You will have to find a new doctor, James."

Right then it dawned on me. Dr. Weston K. Flank had me. He had me good and scared, bare-assed in a stark-white hospital gown with little bluebirds on it. I kept calling him *Wes* because I knew it would make him uncomfortable. That was rude, and now he was fucking with me—soldiers, post-traumatic stress, frozen neurons, what an elaborate ruse. He really did have me. I was just hanging there in space, like a piñata stuffed with stars, and all Dr. Weston K. Flank had to do to shatter my universe was close his eyes and swing. I had to justify this injustice!

"Wes, I'm sorry," I said. "Just tell me what is really going on."

"Sorry for what, James?"

"For being a dick and calling you *Wa-a-a-es*."

"I don't think you're a dick, James. Call me Wes if you like."

"No, you definitely do."

"Trust me, I don't."

"You're fucking with me."

"No, James, I am not *fucking with you*."

"I am not a goddamn piñata!"

"I never said you were."

"But you're fucking with me!"

"I am not, James. Relax now. Withdrawal is hard. We'll make it as easy as possible."

"Easy?"

"Yes, now just relax."

"You're fucking with me, you goddamn koala!" I yelled, pointing my index finger at him. I then tried to push myself free from my metal bed to confront him, maybe rattle his cage a bit. However, Wes, who played two seasons as linebacker for Notre Dame back in the sixties, back when ball was its grittiest, thwarted this effort relatively easily. He grabbed me by the shoulders of my hospital gown just as the tips of my toes were pressing into the cold linoleum floor. He forced his chlorine eyes upon my tired orbs and said, "I AM NOT FUCKING WITH YOU!"

And sadly, even in all my madness, I could tell he was indeed "not fucking with me." Heavy, out of breath and fight, I conceded. "I am sorry I called you Wes," I pleaded, and I really meant it.

"I know. It's okay, call me Wes," he replied, fixing his white coat.

"Well, thank you, Wes. *Wes*, shit. I am sorry. Thank you, Doctor Wes, Doctor Weston, uh, I mean Mr. Fl-a-a..." I stuttered, feeling a wave of tiredness sweep over me as my world began to spin.

"It's okay, J-a-a-a-ammmess." Wes spoke softly. "How about you lie down and we bring in another IV? You look really faint; it's a lot to digest."

His voice drifted elsewhere as my mind began stuttering like a rusted jalopy. "Thank you, Doctor Flank W-e-st-on..." The avalanche of sleep was creeping up on me again. The red Sun had set, and a cool breeze let in from a small crack in the window guided me back down flat onto my bed. I could faintly make out Wes's voice calling for the little nurse just over the strumming of my roommate's breathing machine as I began to chase that little ball of yarn back into the cradle of my mind.

CHAPTER
— 22 —

Spiraling down through a galaxy of blackness, I awoke with a heavy thud perfectly cross-legged by a fire, sky-high in spirit, and my stomach heavy with sugar cookies and eggnog. As the darkness drew from the corner of my eyes, I put a finger to my nose just a little late. "You!" sang Lucia and Eli in unison like two good lovers, like two mourning doves. Damn, it was good to see them together again. I loved them both. I loved them there, sitting before the fire in our cozy modern cave. I loved them watching the burning embers dance like gypsies, Lucia drinking wine, Eli drinking whiskey, a half-completed Scrabble board between them.

I had lost at *nose goes,* comatose and slow, caught between love and the primal laziness a warm fire brings. I had to go across the estate to get Doris from the guest residence. I did not mind. We always played charades on Christmas—or at least we used to. It had been difficult of late, Eli and I sporadically chasing women, cars, and spaceships, Doris working alone on her novel.

"And James," Lucia smiled, "can you ask Doris to bring me down a scarf? I left mine at Sara's." I noticed the nape of her neck was bare. She was wearing an oversized blue sweater, patterned with falling snowflakes.

"Yeah, you see the girl had no time," Eli said as he stared into the fire. "I swooped her off her feet real quick. No time, my man... no time, my man." Eli laughed, his beard strong and red-brown like a forest fox. He lifted the bottle from his lap. I watched as he pulled from the whiskey and spat a little bit into the fire, the flames up and roaring. The three of us howled and turned 'round on the hardwood floor. When we came to a rest, Lucia locked eyes with me, her eyes deep and mysterious like blue river rocks. "Oh, but you know that's not true, James."

"It is! It is!" shouted Eli with a *satisfied* crooked smile.

"Oh, but it is not!" Lucia looked at me again with her big drooping blues. "You know where I found him?" She tilted her head toward Eli, whose arms were free, hands calm in his lap with the bottle. He was posed like a Buddha, eyes like jewels, staring deep into the belly of the fire. "I found him shit-faced outside of The Jive!"

"No time, James." Eli said with a smile, pleased with himself, "No time, my man, no time to pack the scarf!"

Lucia shook her head and smiled softly; she was so kind. "He was reading poems out loud with some prime San-Fran bums. James, I'll tell ya, you got a real beauty for a brother." I really did.

Still, I couldn't help thinking Lucia was even more beautiful, her skin so fair and innocent, like fresh snowfall, and her lips red and moving like fall apples.

"You see, he came by Sara's place," Lucia said. "I was at the market, and Sara done told him off, told him to go, told him to get gone. Told him I had found a new lover with a twelve-inch snake!"

"Twelve!" shouted Eli, still not facing us, crisscross-applesauce with a huge grin on his face.

"So Eli went straight to the bottle, all torn up! You know why, James?"

"Because he's a Buffalo?"

"No, because he loves me!"

"I do, I do," Eli nodded.

"And of course, when Sara told me what she had done, I had to find him! I went to damn near fifteen bars before I found him out in the alley behind The Jive around midnight. Ain't that something? Drivin' all the way up to San Francisco on a whim. I knew it was love."

"It's all love," I said and smiled, watching a thin strand of blonde hair snowflake silently across Lucia's forehead. It came to rest on the ridge of her tiny nose as she reached to rearrange some letters on the Scrabble board. I wanted to brush it back, but I didn't. Instead she blew it out of her way with one warm breath, and this reminded me of Mary Ann Lewis. Mary Ann Lewis always did that. I remembered how Lucia had kissed me on the beach; I still felt terrible for that. I wanted to tell Eli, though I knew I never would.

"I understand you almost made up, too, with . . . what's her name?" Lucia said, interrupting my thinking, my thinking of what she probably never thought of. It was good that way.

"Uh, yeah," I slurred. "Mary Ann Lewis." I wondered if Eli had kissed Mary Ann when I left. I wondered if she had kissed him. I would never know. It was good that way. It had to be.

"You ran, yes?"

"Yeah, I ran."

"Why'd you run? Was it out of love?"

"I ran out of, uh, something, I suppose." *I ran out of gas*, I thought. "But I'm good now in big America; my brain's a dream."

"I'm sorry, honey."

"Don't be. I still got King."

"Ooooh! I love that little guy," cooed Lucia.

King wasn't that little anymore. His paws were big and clumsy. It was kind of sad. Though I suppose he was never that little anyway, always so big in spirit. "Yeah, I still got King," I laughed, pulling on the sleeves of my sweater.

"Where is that little bastard?" shouted Eli, who was still meditating by the fire, warm with whiskey and love.

"King! EEE-oooooo," I howled and turned away from Lucia, who was still twisting a few letters around on the Scrabble board, her skinny fingers directing a ballroom dance with the alphabet. In a matter of seconds, I could hear the scampering of larger paws coming in from the kitchen, followed by the emergence of King's spotted face around the corner.

I let out another "EEEE-oooooo" and braced myself as King started his engine, his big paws struggling to gain traction on the hardwood floor before bolting into motion. In three large bounds he was upon us, and he had to throw on his brakes after working so hard to gain momentum. Clumsy, he was late in doing so. He spun past me and into the half-completed Scrabble board, letters flying every which way. We laughed and laughed. King panted heavily with excitement, the corner of his mouth open as if to say, *Shucks guys, I did it again.*

I stood up and grabbed a jacket from the closet and motioned for King to grab my boots from the foot of the stairs. He did so happily, his mouth salivating at the taste of real leather.

"Don't forget to ask for a scarf!" shouted Lucia, who was struggling to gather the Scrabble pieces back together in the center of the board.

Assuring her I would not, I stood up and headed for the door. I whistled for King to follow me, and he did so with my boots in his mouth, wagging his tail. I looked down at Lucia. Her skinny fingers were once again dancing across the Scrabble board. Her head was turned down, a streak of blonde hair swaying in motion. With a heavy heart, I headed toward the door, eyeing the guest residence through the window, where a light was glowing faintly upstairs. As I moved forward, I looked down, and my eyes caught some Scrabble letters that had been spun across the wood floor. They were arranged:

GO D JOB KEEP GOING

Startled, I jumped back, and I felt a sharp pain in the arch of my left foot. I looked down and realized the line was incomplete. The missing piece was painfully digging into my bare foot. I slid the tiled letter into the gap completing the word score with my big toe. The letters when perfectly aligned read:

GOOD JOB KEEP GOING

Good job keep going. I rubbed my eyes and looked back down at my naked feet pressing against the cold hardwood. The message was still there, bold as ever on tiny ivory-colored squares. I closed my eyes again, and when I opened them the tiles were gone. All of the blocks were accounted for and back on the Scrabble board, where Eli and Lucia had resumed their game fireside. Perhaps my brain wasn't such a dream. Or perhaps my brain was too much of a dream. King dropped my boots on the floor. He then looked up at me curious as to why we had stopped. I bent over and picked up the boots, once again peering out through the window as a light flickered in the distance. I looked back across the floor expecting to see the lettered game pieces perfectly aligned. There were no letters to be found; however, the message was clear.

CHAPTER
— 23 —

Out through the living room French doors, King and I were spat onto the back lawn. We were faced with thick reeds of wild grass almost head high. Eli and I really did need to hire some gardeners now that I was home again. Perhaps that was why Doris had been so distant lately—she couldn't make it to the house anymore, the grass was too high. What a jungle.

In my back pocket, I found a lighter and pulled a cigarette from the pack resting in my front shirt pocket. The winter air was thick and heavy, a treat of the season, each breath going down cold like a scoop of vanilla ice cream. The stars were hanging high and sharp in the sky. I lit my fag and graciously welcomed the warm smoke into my lungs. I would need more light to make it through the tall grass. A thin purple cloud was arcing across the moon, casting an eerie shadow over the entire estate. I was sure once I was inside of the tall grass I would probably not be able to see my own, uh, well, I would not be able to see much.

I found an old wooden shed wedged between the tall grass and the side of the house. I had never been in the shed. Truthfully, I hardly remembered it being there along the side of the house. Inside the shed, there was an old oil-burning lantern amongst the dust and smell of stale sweat. The lantern surprisingly took only a second to light. Eli must have used it recently. The oil bowl was full, and it was the only item inside the small wooden shed that wasn't caked in dust. Next to the lantern, I found a box of matches bearing the initials *C.D.B.* and a tiny gold buffalo in the upper right corner. I had seen these before. They were my father's, Charles David Buffalo's matchboxes. The kitchen cabinets were still filled with them. Eli used them all the time, even though we both hated Charles David Buffalo. I was never sure why, perhaps he just didn't care and he needed the matches, or perhaps Eli missed the old bastard. Anyway, he always needed them. I mean he lit his cigarettes with sticks, and he usually broke three or four before he could catch a flame. He was always too excited. Still, he loved the style, the style of lighting a cigarette with a match. I did, too.

I pulled one of the sticks from the box and struck a flame on my first try. I pushed the flame to the lantern and watched as it danced and the wick flickered to life, the inside of the shed humbly glowing brighter. There was not much to see, just an old mower with three wheels, a bucket filled with dirt-stained gloves, fertilizer, mouse droppings, seeds that looked like mouse droppings, and a scattered assortment of gardening tools. I grabbed a hoe from the pile of tools, figuring it would help me keep the grass away from my face.

Feeling claustrophobic, I stepped out into the fresh air of the night, the red-rusted door hinges on the shed crying for mercy as I slammed the door with a thunderous clap. King heard the shed door close and came trotting in from the fringe of the tall grass, his ears erect at the promise of adventure.

There was no easy way to enter the wall of green, so we just went in head on, King leading the way, I following shortly behind, swinging the hoe to clear a path in the reeds. A few feet inside the thicket it grew dark. I could vaguely make out the light flickering far in the window of the guest residence. After ten yards or so it was gone. Heavy clouds rolled in, obliterating the stars and the moon. Eventually it was completely dark. No heavenly lights for me that night. No, my lantern was the only light I had.

Thirty yards or so in, my eyes began to sting as the dormant pollen and all sorts of bugs came to life in the night as we pushed through the reeds. I could hear the crickets chirping and the scampering of small animals moving away from us. King let out a loud howl. The air was thick and cold, but it was itchy too. Determined, I lowered my head and let King continue to lead the way. Soon after, my eyes began to sting, and my throat began to itch unbearably from the inside out. Eventually the itching crawled into my chest, and I started to cough and wheeze. I pulled my jacket high up around my mouth and continued to brush the grass aside blindly with the hoe.

The lawn of the Buffalo estate had turned into an urban jungle. I began to question if I should head back. I should have phoned Doris, though she would have never answered; she always unplugged the phone or left it off the hook. King was doing fine. I wasn't, my eyes were burning red. My vision had become impaired as well, flickering in and out like an old black-and-white television, my head throbbing as I could feel the veins in the whites of my eyes bulge. For a while it was hard for me to see much of anything at all. I had lost connection; my eyelids were shooting off like the shutter on a broken camera, revealing nothing but the static movement of grass.

I kept stumbling forward until I almost stepped on King, who had come to an abrupt stop. I figured the reeds were getting to him, too. I knew if we were going to make it, I would have to keep pushing, so I closed my eyes tight and swung the hoe feverishly at the tall grass.

Wwhhhaannnggg.

My hands stung with vibrations all the way up to my elbows, and I instantly fell to the ground. Dazed and practically blind, I stared up through the grass and at the garden hoe, which was suspended in midair amongst the reeds and jumping bugs. I got up, shaking loose the porcupine feeling in my arms. I was able to trace the wooden end of the hoe down to the metal base, which had sunk deep into the trunk of a tree.

I knew exactly where we were.

I pushed the grass away and ran my hands up and down the bark of the tree like a blind man learning to read braille. I couldn't help but laugh madly in the night. King let out another loud bark. I put my arms around the tree, laughing madder and madder as I scaled my way around its large trunk. On its green north side I knelt down and brushed away the moss at the bottom of the trunk until I could feel the intricate ridges of the bark. I laughed, running my fingers through the crooked familiar curves as if it were the spine of an old lover. I kept going until my fingers were wedged deep in the cold damp earth.

Relaxed with a strange sense of familiarity and direction, I sat down, my back against the tree, and kicked the reeds away with my boots, clearing a bit of space. I could taste the clear sky through my throbbing eyes, the purple clouds covering the moon had moved on, and a slow calm fell over the reeds; the night was still again.

The little clearing I had created allowed my eyes to cool with the fresh air, and my nose stopped running a bit. I pulled the pack of cigarettes from my shirt pocket, along with the matches I had found in the shed. King's head rested down on my lap. I lit up and allowed myself to get lost in the night's sky, following the stars, scattered like sea glass. I saw them for what they were—beautiful fragments washed across the atmosphere.

I heard a scampering of what sounded like a small animal farther north of us in the grass. I dragged on my cigarette and thought nothing of it. King, on the other hand, lifted his head, letting out a growl and showing some teeth. I grabbed the fur of his neck to tell him to stay put. "Let's stay together, buddy." I coughed, exhaling smoke from my mouth, closing my eyes, tears running down the side of my face from the excess exposure to itchy things.

The tobacco smoke soothed my burning lungs, and if I hadn't known better, I probably could have taken a nap against the old familiar tree. A Pacific winter's breeze came rolling off the ocean, moving my dirty hair about, kissing my burning face. I could have stayed there for hours and listened to the crickets singing and the surf banging its rhythmic drum on the cliffs below. However, when I pressed my ear, I swear I could hear the grass whispering, *job keep going, good job keep going.* "Do you hear that?" I said to King. He seemed annoyed we had stopped for so long. He just buried his nuzzle into the dirt and let out a sigh.

When the cold from the ground began to seep up through my jeans I decided it was time to move on. King happily bounced to his feet. I was less excited about the prospect of reentering the reeds. I ran my hands once more through the tree's bark, moss gathering underneath my fingernails. I slowly circled back around its base to remove the hoe, which was still suspended in midair amongst the reeds of grass and tiny flying bugs. My boots crunched against the cold earth. In the matted grass I found my lantern, which had blown out, its glass shattered. I tried a couple of times to light it, first with the matches and then with my lighter, but nothing struck. The oil must have leaked out.

Again, I could hear scampering in the grass ahead. Most likely a rabbit, but it could also have been a coyote, so I needed King to stay close. King was not smart when it came to things like that. He could bring me my boots when I asked, yet he would turn himself into a meal if given the chance. He was too friendly to be smart. King could easily be drawn into a trap chasing one of the smaller coyote females for miles, thinking he had found a friend, jumping along until his big clumsy paws waltzed right into a coyote den. I couldn't help him then.

The noise grew louder and I could hear what sounded like a faint jog deep in the grass. I was pretty sure this was not a rabbit. My heart dropped into my stomach, and I reached down for King's collar, but it was too late.

Swwsshhhhhhh.

The movement in the grass ahead drew closer, and King could not resist. He took off, leaving me standing alone, dead lantern in hand.

"King!" I whispered, my voice hoarse in panic.

It was no use. I could hear him running wildly in the brush. I turned quickly to grab the hoe. I pulled it from the trunk just as everything went bright white in a horrific flash! Then my world turned completely black as I felt a sharp pain erupt through the side of my head. I fell to the ground, my face pressing into the damp earth, and could hear King barking in the distance.

I caught my breath and felt my ribs crunch as a pointed toe wedged into my side, rolling me over flat on my back. My eyes no longer blinked like shutters; now they were just all broken and out of focus.

The hard pressing of boots on the winter ground thumped up and through my sunken chest. I struggled to gain my wits and guts, trying to match my eyes with a figure as it delivered a subtle kick into the sole of my foot, checking my vitals. My knee twisted outward like a broken levy, and the itching in my lungs coughed up a tiny stream of blood and bad spit.

"Yu gon' be alright, boy," a man snarled.

I could make out a blur of grass and a strange devil standing over me, the tip of his cigarette glowing like the North Star, a bottle in his hands, putrid stink on his breath. The top half of his face was hidden deep in the shadow of the reeds, his crooked teeth and thick chin bathed in moonlight. The figure drew a thin, ivory hand from out of the reeds and wrapped his mouth around a bottle. The man swished the alcohol patiently back and forth in his mouth. I could make out what was most likely my blood dripping from the bottle. It reminded me of the pain in my temple, and I collapsed backward again, my head cushioned by the matted grass.

I could hear the pacing of feet as warm blood slowly trickled from the side of my face through my dirty hair. The stars above blurred together as if someone had smudged a painting of the heavens. A black shadow eclipsed my upward view. I could smell hot whiskey breath as what appeared to be an old man rummaged through my pockets. He took my cigarettes and the matchbox from my front shirt pocket.

"Gahmmuthafuckd," he said, and I could hear him pacing in the grass. I cracked an eye open, sizing up his silhouette amongst the reeds and moonlight. I watched as he removed something from his back pocket. Once again he hovered over me.

"Goohan look naw, I ain't gonna hurdt nawthin," he said and poured some whiskey on his handkerchief while pressing a knee onto my chest. He began to dab timidly at the blood from my forehead, like a spring deer licking salt, exhaling smoke out the side of his mouth. His brimmed hat hid his features, and long silver hair fell across his shoulders and tickled my face, long silver quills dipping into my blood, writing a strange sad story in the tall grass.

I was not keen on being a salt lick, and as soon as enough feeling came into my body, I laid a good one into the side of his crooked nose. I heard a small crack as the drunk fell back a few feet. His bottle flew and shattered against the tree, leaking fire like my lantern leaked its oil. I could briefly make out his face, grey and wrinkled by an expression of pain as he fell.

I inched backward into the reeds like a crab edging into the surf, feeling around for the hoe.

"Gahhhdammn, calm dawhn!" yelled the night devil as I flexed my arms. I extended my fingers in desperation, feeling around for the hoe's wooden handle. His outline grew larger against the night sky as he began to move toward me. I stretched and stretched. I had to be close to the hoe. I could feel nothing. I kept pulling up grass as he drew in on me. I dug at the base of the reeds with my fingernails scratching soil but came up empty-handed. The figure in the night seemed to be in no rush, and he removed his cowboy hat to let his hair fall free in the night, kicking his way through a mess of glass, which crunched like cracking ice beneath his boots.

My heart jumped back to life as I reached back into the reeds, catching the tip of something hard as he inched forward. Out of breath, I drove my hand farther and farther into the grass, my sweaty palm sliding across a wooden handle. Adrenaline pumped through my veins like a shot of electricity as I felt the hoe in my hands. My vision sharpened in like a stone arrow.

Flat on my back, I waited, breathless in anticipation, every hair on my body erect. Completely still, I was the snake in the grass ready to strike. A strange smile crept across my face. I was shamefully going to enjoy this. I was going to lace this old bum. I was the coyote and he was walking into my den.

So I waited as the dumb figure floated across the reeds, and when I got my chance I up and swung with all my might!

I felt the adrenaline seep from my body like a deflating balloon, my emotions erratically flying about. The man dodged the hoe like a seasoned city pedestrian avoiding a bicycle messenger. Anticlimactically, the hoe and my arm fell slowly across my body and stuck upright in the dirt beside me.

The man laughed hysterically, and I felt my heart burrow deeper and deeper into the ground. I could see his head bowed low, belly bouncing in laughter, the silver hair covering his face turning up in the night with the Pacific wind. I reached back again for the hoe. Humiliatingly enough, I couldn't pull it out of the heavy moist dirt—no leverage, or perhaps not enough strength.

"Calm down, nah," the man said. I could tell he was old, his voice worn down by whiskey, slow and gravel-like from tobacco. "Here, take a drag," he said as he kneeled down and tried to place his half-gone cigarette in my mouth. I let it drop to the ground. The old man sighed. "Ah, thas' no gud," he muttered and stood up to stomp the cigarette with his boot.

He kneeled back over me, spinning the box of matches in his weathered hands. Fully exposed in the cracking moonlight, he parted his steel curtain of hair.

My eyes caught his slender broken face, and I traced his long hair down to two crocodile boots glistening in the moonlight, pressing into the bloody mud and matted grass. I dropped my head, motionless as Charles David Buffalo tapped the matchbox against the tip of my nose and with a laugh whispered, "Did yu mess me, sawn?"

CHAPTER
— 24 —

"Naw, catch your breath, *Ja-a-amess*, owl answa thad for ya," Charles David Buffalo chuckled to himself as he clapped the mud off his crocodile boots, banging his large feet against the moss-covered tree. The dead leaves fell down around me as the tree's trunk collected mud.

"I know ya missd me, sawn," he said, and then paused. His nose turned up in thought, a nose as crooked and deceiving as his smile. I could tell he was at home, a tired cowboy in the moonlit night, arm and elbow against the old willow.

"Naw, I know ya missd me," Charles David Buffalo said. He then coughed into a fist. Even in the cool night his forehead was covered in a heavy sweat. "I know ya missd me," he rattled on, wiping the moisture from his brow. "I know ya missd me, or else you wud't have dun put me here in deez gawdforsaken reeds!"

Charles David Buffalo pushed off the tree and busted his arms wide open, spinning slowly around amongst the tall grass. "LOOK AT DIS PLA-AHH-

ACE!" he screamed in between his large, gut-heaving laughs. "Yu gotd sum imagination, boy!"

I could see Charles David Buffalo just as I had always imagined. There he was, long hair and wild drunk, standing tall in the night, proud and dishonest, in his crocodile boots, leaning against the willow like an old cowboy not ready to concede the West. Proud, in the boots he claimed to kill for, wearing his customary brown leather vest, bloodstained above the heart from where the bullet hit his chest in Jerusalem. Ironically, he claimed to kill for the vest as well. On that night, I danced toe to toe with a notorious murderer of crocodiles, thieves, and Southern Comfort.

"Ha! Yu can't forget me!" he shouted. "Hell, I'm lost in deez reeds as much as you are, Ja-a-aaaems."

Charles David Buffalo still had me from the grave. He was un-living proof that most things never truly die. Most things stay alive in the mind, like a forgotten cowboy keeps to the frontier, his ghost pushing purple sagebrush, his cold wind blowing sand up toward the stars and against the red rocks. Whistling, if you listen, his sick spirit throwing stones, if you look, all just to prove he can still make the desert sing and ripple. So, I stood and listened to Charles David Buffalo laugh hard. I watched as he spun in the reeds. And I smiled as he eventually coughed himself into a broken-down body tizzy. With his chest bloody and pushing slower, the frontier went quiet and the night stood still.

He wanted me to become *well*, sure. The hell he did.

The Will and Testament, Henry P. Whitehouse, the pills—it was all bullshit. I watched as Charles David Buffalo began to spin the rim of his hat around his index finger. Dr. Westin Flank's voice drifted through my head: "Without these scarring memories, the soldier would harbor less anger when they thought about the war—and they would, well, they would be willing to kill again."

I knew then, with little uncertainty, that Charles David Buffalo had been behind the pills. And I knew why he wanted me to take them. He wanted me to kill for him again. He wanted me to fight his egotistical war of self-preservation.

He wanted me to forget what a lousy father he had been. He wanted the world to see me as a reflection of his greatness. He wanted immortality. The inheritance was simply bait used to draw me into his plans. He thought the pills could make up for his absence. He wanted me to smile and one day tell my kids that he, Charles David Buffalo, wasn't such a bad guy. *Sure, your granddaddy was a good ol' guy,* I'd say. *Some say he wasn't but that ain't true! The hell he wasn't, kids! Look what he done, kids! He gave us all these nice things! Here, go play with one of his guns!* He was through and through a narcissist in love with the restoration of his own image, even in death. I hadn't seen things this clear in a long time—I had been walking crop circles trying to please a dead man.

I could feel the dreamy falseness of the winter's ground and the falseness of my bleeding in the grass. Still, it all seemed truthful and clean. I was moving through my mind freely into areas I had previously kept locked shut. My veins flexed rich with moving life. I could taste it all. I touched my flesh, I could feel the IV wedged into my forearm.

I knew Charles David Buffalo's Will and Testament was withdrawing. Fast fading was the desire to fill it. I watched his wishes seep out through my mind as the IV calmly dripped in.

My eyes sparked and fell, red, deadly, then hot blue, my eyes burning alive, red, tight, and turning blue, up in flames in big America! I couldn't sleep any longer. So like a bad child, I had decided it was time wake up the entire house. Nose deep and practically blind in my mind, head cut and spilling, swimming in a dream of turning grass, I was moving the entire *Tired Coast*. And I was doing it all, out cold and warm, from my bed at Saint Victoria's Los Angeles Medical.

I was slipping into reality as I fidgeted with the IV in my arm. Behind Charles David Buffalo in the reeds, I could see my roommate, the old sage, smiling and holding hands with the tiny Hispanic nurse, his hospital bed floating peacefully in the reeds. The tiny nurse bent down and kissed him. As their lips locked, tears streaked down the old man's cheeks, cutting clear through his thin goatee. His breathing machine humming, his heart beating loudly, like Charles David

Buffalo's feet rapping against the old willow. Minutes passed before the little nurse again caught my eyes locked with the old man's. Blushing, she grabbed the reeds and slid them shut like she had previously with the blue curtain, the two lovers disappearing behind the tall green grass.

As I stared at the wall of dancing green, where the nurse and the old man had disappeared, I couldn't help but smile from ear to ear. I could feel my mind clicking in no particular way. It was clicking naturally; goodness, what other way could it click! My mind was singing and flowing free, like snow melting off the highest peak and running into a new buck's mouth.

I was the sound, and I was the light, and I was certain then that I could in fact hear someone singing beyond the reeds.

I stood and smiled at Charles David Buffalo, who was leaning against the tree exposed as a faker, as a fraud, his ghost-like figure growing pale in my mind's moonlight. "I wantch'ya to naw sumthin." I spoke fat-cheeked, clumsy, doing my best to mimic the accent I had given him. "I still thank yu real hur, evan though dis is in muh, uh...," I paused, looking up toward the light flickering in the guest residence, "... my head," I finished, my voice falling as quiet as a field mouse.

"Well, da fuck I am, boy!" yelled Charles David Buffalo as he slid his hat back on to his head, taming his long silver hair, silver hair that would have almost been invisible if it wasn't for my bloodstains at its tips.

"I know." I did my best to look down and keep my eyes away from him, drawn to the light burning in the guest residence. "I know I put you here," I whispered as he flickered in and out of my haunted existence.

I played with the IV, pushing it back and forth in my arm, and like a light switch, I was shifting Charles David Buffalo across the visible spectrum of light. The fiddling of my forearm caused Charles David Buffalo and the dancing reeds to become increasingly transparent, like fog receding in front of the hot Sun, while the hospital room, my inevitable shore, grew ever present. Looking down, I could see my gown with the tiny little bluebirds on it and my squirming bare feet as the lukewarm ceiling lights outshined the heavenly sky. I slid the needle back into place and watched as it seemingly melted and disappeared back into my flesh.

I hadn't anticipated that.

I felt my forearm and instantly regretted the decision, clawing and digging at the skin where my naked veins lay, begging to pull the IV, begging to go back, out of the reeds, away from Charles David Buffalo. It was too late, and my digging was futile. I couldn't find the switch anymore, no escape from the yard, and no retreat into the doghouse, nowhere to bury my nasty bones.

"Ya so go doo it now!" shouted Charles David Buffalo. Through the corner of my eyes, I could see faint tears sliding down his pink jellyfish cheeks, and I almost felt bad for him as he sputtered and sputtered, and I scratched and scratched at my arm. No, neither of us wanted to be there.

"Jus go doo it. Pudt me back out somewhere else deep in your mind where yull neva see meh," Charles David Buffalo wailed, his loose arms flapping in pain at his sides. "I know you hate m-m-mehh, so do it, jus dooo it. Kill me off again. I don carrreee! Radther have nawthin than dis existence here. I cand't breathe in deese drudged reeds, James!"

I laughed in desperation. "Yeah, they itch, don't they?"

"Do it!" he screamed again.

"I can't!" I yelled. And that was the truth. I could never free him from the reeds. I wished I could put him somewhere else, anywhere else, keep him hidden, and never return to that place. However, I knew visiting Charles David Buffalo had never and would never be pleasant or avoidable.

"Get me outta here!" he screamed again, his eyes hotter this time, no longer filled with sorrow, steaming red, drunk and mad. "Do it, boi! Or awl do it mahself!" Charles David Buffalo popped up in a rage. He grabbed the metal hoe, briefly feeling its weight in his hand, and started a bad drunk run forward, losing his footing, arms painfully pressing into broken glass.

"ARRRrrgGGHhhhhhhuckkk." He let out a terrible scream. Shards of glass were protruding from his forearms. His hands looked like talons as his fingers clenched open in agony. Roaring in the sparkling night, he got up and once again raised the hoe above his head, taking off toward me in a rush of murderous anger. I could taste the fire on his breath as he drew closer and closer. I started to retreat into the reeds and I stumbled over my nervous feet. Charles David Buffalo saw his opportunity and he planted a boot into my chest. I collapsed to the ground. "Now he say he can't get me out of here!" He shouted, he started to laugh madly again as he stepped over me. "Sorry, son," he said still laughing to himself, "but that jus can't be true."

Charles David Buffalo slowly raised his weapon up above his head. His motion was unstable. His arms moved like old roller-coaster cables, the metal end of the hoe pulling toward the moon in uneven jerks. I held my breath as my father casually straightened his back. He tightened his old arms, pushing the hoe up to its highest extension. A hollow look came over his eyes. He wobbled back and forth. He felt the wood in his hands like the slugger he knew he had always been. *This was it,* I thought. The hoe teetered back and forth across the outline of a full moon. Then it started downward, uneasy in its descent. CDB pushed forward with all his might, and his torso contracted as he did so. Halfway through his swing, his right side buckled in what seemed like a drastic overcompensation. I heard a thump as the hoe pulled right as a result and stuck into the mud a few inches from my forehead.

Charles David Buffalo collapsed to his knees in agony. I thought the old bastard was having a heart attack. I watched curiously as he grabbed the lower part of his leg and began to curse. I saw he was bleeding badly. The denim above his right boot was torn, and his flesh was spewing blood like a broken drainpipe.

"King!" I cried as his spotted face appeared behind the old man. His muzzle was lowered, his teeth exposed, and the hair along his neck stood tall. He had sunk his big teeth into Charles David Buffalo's right calf.

The Dalmatian's tail wagged as he saw me sit upright. He daintily danced his way around the fallen Charles David Buffalo. I sat upright at the foot of the mess I had created. Sweat trickled down my forehead. I could feel a stinging sensation where the hoe should have landed right beneath my matted hairline. I stroked King's lovely spotted neck, as Charles David Buffalo slithered back into the reeds, disappearing as quickly as he had come, leaving nothing behind except a snail's trail of sticky blood. "Fuc-ckkin m-uhh-uht..." I could hear the cowboy's voice trailing off with the wind.

I then looked up at the guest residence, the reason I had ventured out in the first place. I noticed the light had gone out during my latest tussle with Charles David Buffalo. I picked up the hoe from the ground in case he returned. As I watched the grass sway side to side then eventually go calm, I couldn't help but think about ripples moving on a desert lake. *You can still make the desert sing, old man,* I thought. I then looked at my hands and saw that they were becoming more and more transparent.

In the distance I could still hear Charles David Buffalo's wailing.

I stood, staring at the dark outline of the guesthouse hardly visible along the tops of the reeds, waiting, just waiting for the light to reappear. It did not. And I knew I didn't have much time. I felt a tingling sensation in my arm where the IV was. I decided to take one last shot at the guesthouse. Holding the hoe in front of me like a javelin, I took off violently into the reeds. I ran recklessly and I soon became lost. The reeds were too high, and without the light I had no idea where I was headed. Still, I ran blindly into the night until I couldn't anymore. I stopped, overcome with futility. I let out a scream staring up toward the stars. "I'm ready now!" I yelled. "Doctor Wes, pull it! Just pull it! I am ready to come home!"

King had been following me, and he collided with my heels as I shouted. My cries went unanswered. Dizzy with exhaustion, I pushed the hoe to the side and collapsed into the grass. King sang in the moonlight, feeling my sorrow. He disappeared into the reeds for a few seconds before circling back. He then stood over me and began to lick the salty tears, snot, and dried blood off my face.

I could hear my father again; he was singing softly this time.

I felt compelled to rise and follow his voice; he sounded weak, and I wanted to finish him. He had cost me Doris.

I grabbed the hoe and let King lead us westward through the reeds, trailing the scent of blood while I listened to the sound. "I know you can hear that!" I said to King. And soon, I could hear the ocean as well. I started to run again. I was certain we were drawing closer as the hymn grew louder, found between thundering claps of the surf. The wind rose and tossed my tears and wild hair beneath the star maps. The grass eventually wore thin, and the singing became more audible. King stopped in front of me as we peered out through the thin grass. I could make out a figure glowing in the night. "This is good-bye," I whispered to King, feeling the weapon in my hand.

I stepped through the grass and felt the hoe slip from my hands, landing without a sound in the night. There she was, bathed in light, her heels teetering off the edge of the bluffs, the surf below rapping loudly against cliffs, causing the earth to quake and shudder much like my heart.

Doris smiled. She was more beautiful than I had remembered. She was holding a bouquet of yellow roses against her chest. A mist began to rise up from the bluffs as the waves continued to crash. I noticed she was singing, barely moving her small lips. Her head was turned upward, and her oval glasses reflected the night.

Good job keep going, good job keep going, she sang like an angel. I knew then, she had been with me all along.

I stretched to touch her, and my reach was shortened as a tiny hand pressed firmly against my arm. And with a hollow pinch, I felt a tug on the IV as the night's falling stars, the swaying grass, King's cool baying, the willow's ballet leaves, my father, and Doris vanished in a flicker flash. The little Hispanic nurse appeared over me washed in hospital lighting. Looking down at me like the Virgin Mary, she spoke in a heavenly voice. "It's almost over now, James."

CHAPTER
— 25 —

Two weeks later, though, I was beginning to think it had only just begun as I sat outside Saint Victoria's Los Angeles Medical staring at a place across the street called Pink's Showgirls, smoking a cigarette. I was waiting for Eli and Lucia to come and pick me up. I was feeling good enough to let a good-looking, slightly let-go, blond man in large neon-tinted aviators bum a cigarette. The man seemed familiar enough, as he stumbled full drunk at noon across the highway from the strip joint and saw me light up on the outpatient bench.

"Thanks, buddy," he slurred, his chest half exposed and showcasing a gold chain with a pink-and-turquoise flamingo on it. As I looked back across the street, trying to avoid conversation, I noticed the same pink-and-turquoise flamingo painted on the sign beneath flashing lights that silhouetted the outline of a showgirl.

I looked over at the man and tried to place where I knew him from, as he fumbled with my lighter and kicked it into the hospital's cobblestone turnaround as his medallion dangled out in public, swaying side to side. He was comically moving his large body around in the shade of the hospital's large palms.

I laughed. "You're a big fan?"

"Of what?" demanded the chubby blond in a slur, tongue slowed by beer and whiskey, his face turned up defensive.

I motioned across the street toward the glowing sign that sporadically flashed "LIVE NUDES."

"Big fan?" he huffed. He had finally trapped the lighter against the curb with one of his white penny loafers. "I own the fucking place."

"That's cool," I replied, chuckling a bit to myself, growing more intrigued with the stranger. He was the first outside man I had spoken to since Dr. Weston K. Flank had declared me medically free, so I added, "How's business?"

"Ha, just fired two of the girls," he said as he calmly lit his cigarette. With a huge smile, he looked up toward the large palms, his dirty-blond hair moving in the wind. "Say, what's your name, compadre?"

"James," I replied.

"Henry Diamonds," he said, his head tilted crookedly. "But you can call me Flynn."

"Hey, Flynn, can I have my lighter back?" I noticed he had accidentally, or on purpose, slid it into his back pocket.

"Oh, yeah, sure, sure, just a habit," he replied, talking too fast, fumbling the lighter toward my feet as he removed it from his pocket. He bent down again, and his loosely buttoned Hawaiian shirt exposed the fold of his large belly, his medallion swinging in the L.A. breeze.

"Say, James, what did they have you for?" He motioned toward Saint Victoria's building. I watched as he shuffled through his pockets, dropping a few track tickets from Santa Anita.

"I was, uh, visiting my father," I said.

"Oh shit, buddy, how's he doing?" he asked.

"Oh, he is just fine, Flynn," I replied.

"Say, you want a lift?" he said with a wink.

"Ha," I said with a laugh. "You shouldn't drive anywhere." I kind of liked the man, even though he was probably someone I couldn't associate with anymore. However, it didn't mean I couldn't at least have a look.

"No, no," he smiled and looked around the outpatient turnaround. "Do you want a *lift*?" He winked again and scratched his nose this time, discreetly pulling a little bag filled with white powder halfway out of his pocket. He motioned toward the dirty strip club, which glowed like a sinner's oasis across the highway.

"I'm good." I must have replied hastily because Henry Diamonds was taken aback a bit, but his good nature soon returned. I imagined that he too fought with the *Bad Dharma*, whether he realized it or not. It didn't matter.

"I just figured you'd want a little something to getchya up after spending some time in there." He motioned toward the hospital again. "It's on me, come on," he said, as happy and excited as a stranger can be.

"Ah, I'm keeping clean, Flynn." I motioned toward the track slips still in his hand. "How are the ponies?"

"Ha," he snorted. "I've got some stuck luck at the moment, *Jaime*."

I laughed. Then it hit me as I studied his strong jawline and wavy blond hair. This was *the man*. The man I had sworn to befriend months ago, the good-natured Buddha from the track, the man who had bet it all on a horse named Sal's Salvation. The same man whom I thought I saw shirtless in the rain outside the Admirals game, smoking a cigarette, all gone in some sort of madness, the man who was raw and reckless, unencumbered and living right and free. So I said with a smile, as he had told me, "Always bet the nines."

And to my greatest disappointment, he replied, "Fuck the nines."

It is awkward to watch your perceptions of people change, whether they were accurate or not. It hurts. Perceptions don't change the present; they change your view of the past, making you feel foolish and cheap, and everything becomes jaded when those cool memories you held onto lose all their meaning and become wrapped inside a terrible false plastic. Henry Diamonds was not the great American Buddha I had hoped for; he was merely a pin of hope I had worn during desperate times. And I could not fault him for his nature; these had been my illusions, not his.

As we stared across the street at Pink's, I started to laugh hysterically as he swayed back and forth on the curb like a cattail caught in the ocean wind. I tried to stop laughing, but I couldn't. Then Flynn started to laugh hard, too, as if he had just realized what was so funny, and his bloodshot eyes began to water a little, and I thought for a second that we could all find some sort of strange beauty in this confusion.

"Hey, what do you say you come to Santa Anita with me this afternoon, pal?"

I looked at him through the corner of my eye. "I am not *that man*," I said. And I wasn't.

"That's good, buddy," he replied, and after finishing his cigarette he slapped a large drunk hand on my shoulder. "Well, thanks for grit. I like you, James."

"You don't really know me, Flynn," I said.

"Don't have to," he replied.

I motioned for him to get gone, and he stumbled back across the highway, which thankfully had a gap in traffic. Halfway across the road, he paused and almost lost his footing in the gravel median and started coming back toward me in a funny jog. He arrived out of breath and folded downward with his hands resting on his knees.

"You're not a cop, are you?" he asked, and I laughed, shaking my head. "Good, because if you *are*, then you have to tell me."

"Yeah, I've heard that," I said.

"Good." He sat beside me on the bench, and I held out my open pack before he had the chance to ask for another cigarette.

"You know, if you ever need a job, I always got openings for someone who is *cool*." He motioned down toward the blow in his pocket, then back at the strip club. "I can tell you're cool, James."

"That's not my thing, Flynn," I said.

"No, no, don't you see? It doesn't have to be your *thing*. Fuck, the two girls I let go today, it *was* their *thing*, and you see it's bad that way," he said as he handed the pack back to me and placed the unburned cigarette above his ear, like a pencil.

"Well...," he stuck his hand outward and I shook it. "If you ever change your mind, here is my card."

"Alright," I replied and took the card, having every intention of tossing it as soon as I could.

"You look familiar; have we met before?" he asked.

"Ah, perhaps, during a different life," I said.

"Hmm." He scratched his chest. "And you're not a cop, right?"

"Not a cop," I reassured him.

"My man...," he smiled and ran a big hand through his wavy hair, taking off right as Eli pulled into the turnaround in a lipstick-red Austin Healy convertible. I shoved the card in my back pocket and nodded to Flynn as he shot me the gun with his left index finger. We really had met in a different life. So, I hopped into the back of the convertible, my clean boots easily clearing the side of the car's low frame. I slapped a hand against the smooth exterior, sending us off into sticky Los Angeles.

CHAPTER
— 26 —

Driving down Highway 101, away from the hospital and Pink's Showgirls, with the radio blasting, the top down, and Sun up, I felt like a young kid again. Eli was pushing the pedals while Lucia rode shotgun, wearing a large, floppy hat, drinking a martini. She looked like a movie star. Eli did, too, driving fast in Los Angeles with his machine-gun sunglasses, the palm trees silhouetted by the high Sun. I put my feet up on the leather center console and felt good about myself, even though the circumstances were rather embarrassing, me being mental in a hospital and all, as Lucia and Eli admired my boots.

Lazy in the red convertible, free to move in the Sun and salty wind, I flew a cupped hand out the side of the car and watched as our speed made my arm duck and dive like a dolphin. I was too nervous to ask about what had turned out with Mary Ann Lewis after I split. Still, I couldn't keep it off my mind as Lucia and Eli twisted fingers across the center console, nudging my boots, to kiss at the occasional stoplight. I was envious of them for all the fun they were having, and no matter how good and stable I got, I realized I would soon need the love of a good woman, or at least I would like to have it. I was reprioritizing my needs of late.

As we cruised along Highway 101 near San Clemente, I couldn't resist any longer, and I eventually got the nerve up to ask Eli what had happened with Mary Ann Lewis. He pulled over to the side of the road and onto some pavement covered with gravel, the car's tires groaning and coming to an abrupt crunching halt. Eli got out of the car in a lazy hop and circled around back, digging in the trunk for a minute or two.

"Here," he said and tossed me a tiny flat brown package that was about the size of a sand dollar. He jumped over the front door into the tan-leather driver's seat. "I was supposed to give this to you the moment I saw you. Guess I was a little late."

"What is it?" I asked, pressing my fingers into the tiny ridges of the package.

"Mary Ann wasn't upset, you know," he replied, ignoring my question.

"She should be," I said as I fumbled with the package.

"Well, she was," Eli turned, flashing a bright smile in my direction, his wavy hair turning up and over. Lucia sat casual with her back to me, staying impartial by pressing her tiny red lips to her martini glass, which turned upward to the Sun, catching Eli's attention.

"Put that fucking thing down while we're stopped!" he said. "James just got out of the hospital, and I am sure he wants to get home, and so do I, so we're not letting some highway ham book us now, okay? Just wait a second."

Lucia just giggled and poured her drink into a Del Taco cup she found on the floor and continued her drinking. I noticed tiny beads of sweat had formed along her upper lip as the Sun glistened on her fair skin.

"Ah, yeah, Mary Ann," Eli said. "Yeah, she was mad at first. I offered to turn around and take her back, but she wouldn't have it, me chasing this one and all." He put a hand on Lucia's thigh. "But after a while she came around, more worried, if anything. Hell, she was still talking about how much she liked you, even when we got to San Francisco."

"Is she still there?" I asked as my heart's compass turned north.

Eli's high crescent smile waned, and I could tell Mary Ann Lewis had hit the bricks. "Ah, no, no, sorry, man. I don't know where she is. I mean she said something about Mexico, but I wouldn't count on it. It seemed like a crock of shit to me. I pressed her for the truth, but she wouldn't budge."

"But you know she left?" I asked.

"Yeah, yeah, she showed up at Sara's, where Lucia and I were crashing just after we had gotten the news about you. I told her what had happened, and she started to tear up a little. She left and returned an hour later with this." He nodded at the package. "She said to give it to you."

"She just left?"

"Afraid so. She had all her luggage with her."

"Mexico!"

"James—"

"And King!"

"She had the dog with her, too."

"Mexico!"

"She is not in Mexico, James. I mean, come on."

"But she said—"

"She must have said that because she didn't want you to know where she went. Okay? Don't get any ideas," Eli said sternly. "If she was down there right now, she would get her pretty little head wrung by the crazy-ass Cartel, and so would you, sooo just sit calm, okay? And open that package; maybe it will say something more."

I tore open the brown paper and at first nothing came out. *What a cruel fucking joke!* I thought. Then a tiny bundle of leather string dropped into my lap. I was hoping for a letter or a short message of sorts. However, there was no paper other than the wrapping. I untangled the mess of thin leather, turning the band straight across my hands, and my heart warmed when I saw dangling from the dark band a tiny silver buffalo. I twisted the metal with my fingertips, and on the back I saw it was engraved:

P. A.

I couldn't make any sense of it. My mind raced with possibilities, slight and running large. Did Mary Ann leave me a cryptic message, the initials P.A. marking a great city? Had I missed something she said about Mexico? No letter! Just a goddamn cryptic message! Why must she be so cruel? So I thought for a while as cars and big trucks moved along the highway. Eventually, I managed to collect my wits. It was simple. Mary Ann Lewis had given me what I hadn't given her. The necklace was a good-bye.

I had been cruel. I had been cruel to Mary Ann Lewis, and I had also been cruel to myself with years of this torturous thought.

I put the band around my neck so that it was visible for all to see. It was a nice charm and nothing more, a charm I liked very much. Besides, chances were that Mary Ann Lewis had bought the necklace secondhand, and she had no choice but to accept the calamity of an ill-engraved buffalo. I laughed to myself at the irony, because I, too, was an ill-engraved Buffalo, and, man, did it feel great to be anything at all. I thrust my chest out to the Sun and let out a large howl.

"I like it!" said Lucia and Eli in unison.

And I liked it even more so because it wasn't perfect.

I felt good and I even laughed and forgot about the letters P.A. for a bit. Then Eli turned toward Lucia and gave her a subtle nudge with his elbow. "Hey, babe, you get it? She gave him a buffalo and our last name is Buffalo, huh, huh?"

We all shared a laugh at what we thought was Lucia's expense as Eli put his foot on the accelerator and crunched the gravel on the side of the highway once more. Yes, we laughed at the blonde, sure, though in reality the laughs were not at Lucia's expense. No, something or someone else had to be picking up our tab because we all felt fine in the Sun and sadness of *Los Angeles*.

"Hey!" I screamed as we quickly gained speed, changing lanes. "What happened to our van?"

"Ha!" Eli kept his face forward as he pressed the gas pedal harder, the engine purring. "I sold that piece of shit."

I thought nothing of it at first.

A few miles outside of the city, though, I realized that everything was changing as Eli and Lucia told me they were going to start enjoying their wealth, convinced America had made its people poor purely out of fashion.

"You see, James," Lucia started in. "In America, it's cool to dress like a bum and wear dirty shoes when you don't have to. Wear holes in your denim for dirty-fashion's sake, never shave, never shower, look like you've got nothing, become the multimillion-dollar software designer that looks unemployable. It's gross. We saw so much of that in San Francisco, it was sickening, and to think that's where the new America's art supposedly comes from: trust-fund babies living purposefully meager. If you're a trust-fund baby, you live, baby!" She dug her nails into Eli's thigh.

I squirmed as she said "trust-fund baby," and Lucia could tell the phrase left me uncomfortable. "Not that the two of you are like that. The two of you are so smart; fuck, it would just be nice to live life without being judged. It's like society wants you to eat cheap and scoff at people in nice diners and restaurants, metaphorically speaking, of course."

Of course! I thought.

"And, James, it's all just a show. It's all just a way to lower expectations. I understand this now." She placed a hand on Eli's shoulder. "We understand this now."

"It's true," Eli said, and turned around while pushing his foot heavy against the accelerator. "And I think now more than ever would be a good time for you to take over your half of the fortune. I have already talked to a good lawyer, and based on what your doctor said about the drugs you were given, we have a solid case that Charles David Buffalo and *his* Doctor, uh, Doctor—what's that fucker's name?"

"Doctor Whitehouse."

"Yeah, I never liked that bastard. It's fucking insane, criminal, I tell you! What do you say, buddy? Let's get at it now, get your money back, no more visits, be free to do what you want? It's as good a time as ever."

"As good a time as ever," I said.

"Perfect, because Lucia and I were thinking about going to France for a little bit, where things are different. You know, forget about all this shit." He waved his hand in no particular direction. "That way we don't have to worry about wiring money or anything like that."

"We're going to fuck in the ocean!" screamed Lucia, and she threw her hands up and out of the convertible.

It was fine with me. I sat calm, my hands folded neatly behind my head, taking the breeze on my teeth. From time to time, I ran my fingers over the silver buffalo hanging from my neck. I could care less. I wanted to straighten things out with Charles David Buffalo's legal team anyway. And I never wanted to see old Doctor Henry Whitehouse again. I never wanted to sit in his office and talk about the changing of his wallpaper, which changed as frequently as my thoughts; we would overanalyze both. So, I just smiled at the two of them in the front seat, all high and mighty on their good fortune. They couldn't have been back together for more than two weeks, though they had changed so much in that time. Two weeks was the length of my stay at the hospital. The time it took me to completely withdraw. I had hoped I had changed, too, and I thought I had. I was feeling real again, raw as dog meat and showing happy teeth.

So on and on things went. We rode down Highway 101, pulling through good space, Eli and Lucia destined to live well; I destined to, well, live. There was no more discussion of wealth from the front, and I was quiet in the back. As the Sun set purple, red-pink, yellow, and glowing across the coast, I waved to a young child who was half asleep with a stuffed bear in the back of an old green Suburban. Her mother and father were driving safe and slow, as they should, and we passed them by before the young girl could wave back.

When the Sun had disappeared and we were closer to home, the headlights on the red convertible dragged and trapped small yet adequate sections of pavement in bright-white light, scattering small rabbits, occasionally lighting up the eyes of a brave deer peering from the heavy pines as we ascended toward the estate. Lucia said she always wanted a deer-fur of some sort, and now that she didn't care about what everyone else thought, she was going to get one. I liked her so much better when she was dishing out shots with a wink in her cute little leopard mask at the Chrysanthemum Ball. She was so innocent and drifting. And I liked Eli better, too, when he was just a wild kid pretending to fly across the shoreline right before Lucia kissed me on the lips. I liked myself less then, and at that moment I liked myself better than either of them as I sat calm in the back seat. I looked away every time we drove by a pass and a deer's eyes lit up all green in front of the convertible's beams. And I looked away as Eli pretended to cock a shotgun with his single right hand like the Terminator, and I thought of the silent desert wind every time Lucia shouted, "BOOM!"

Yes, things were changing. I didn't really like the two of them anymore, even though they both hugged me and cried real tears when I came down and fell into their arms at the bottom of the guest residence, some hours later, spilling a box of Doris's possessions across the flat pavement.

Doris was dead. She had died three years earlier from a bad cancer. Her death was and will always be my greatest heartbreak. I thought about the day when I jumped off the tree house a lot lately, the day I realized she would never sit with me again. I was deemed unwell shortly after. And perhaps I wasn't well, then, or now, but on the long drive home, as I looked at Eli and Lucia making big plans in the front seat, I couldn't help but wonder who was *well*. Charles David Buffalo had felt as though he had failed *himself* in producing a son who was "un-well." I had caused him some embarrassment. I was beginning to see this as an accomplishment. I was happy to have failed the old bastard; he wasn't that great of a man. So I had sat in silence as the three of us drove back to the estate. I was ready to visit the guesthouse.

In the start of my dreaming at Saint Victoria's, I had promised Lucia that I would bring her one of Doris's scarves after she had lost hers up in San Francisco. I promised her that as she was moving her fingers nimbly across a Scrabble board, so pretty and free. I brought her Doris's scarf without her asking, as she was moving her fingers furiously across a Blackberry. I realized Lucia had lost much more than a scarf up in San Francisco. She had lost her fucking mind. Eli, too. Still, I brought her Doris's scarf. And I gave Eli a faded Polaroid of the three of us: him, Doris, and me, looking curiously up from a book Doris had laid across her lap some years earlier when we were safe in the tree house. It was labeled in neat female handwriting, *Tinkerbelle & the Lost Boys.* Maybe they could see, like me, how nice she was. Much nicer than anything else I could imagine, and maybe they would grow to feel her like I felt her then, clutching the last of her possessions. I no longer envied them, and I was happy in my own skin, running a hand across my silver buffalo, thinking of all the great things I could and would do. I was proud of my heavy heart.

CHAPTER
— 27 —

When I first got back to the Tired Coast I was more depressed than ever. They say it is "natural" when withdrawing from antidepressants. It seems weird to use the word "natural" when referring to something as unnatural as a chemical withdrawal.

Dr. Weston Flank had called one night and suggested I join a therapy group for people recovering from prescription drugs. "Similar drugs, Wes," I said, "like what, pain-killers or something like that?" He said he was in fact referring to something of that nature. I told him to "go eat a dick." Then I hung up before he could argue. A few minutes later I felt bad, so I called him back and politely declined. I was "still feeling pretty testy," I said. And I clenched my teeth when he responded by telling me that it was "perfectly natural."

Speaking of things that made my teeth clench, Eli and Lucia were nice enough to hang around the estate for the rest of the month. They passed the time fighting and having sex. Eventually they departed for France at the beginning of February. I'm pretty sure they stayed to make sure I didn't kill myself.

Ironically, I felt a lot better when they left.

I had bought a three-speed bicycle at a garage sale the previous Saturday. It was old; however, the sea's rust had been kind and stayed off the burnt orange frame. "Just put some air in the tires," the man said as I was pedaling out of his driveway. He had told me he was selling all of his possessions in order to buy a houseboat. I smiled as I rode away. "Good day, Captain!" I shouted, saluting him with my right hand as I weaved playfully in the street. The man laughed.

Things were getting better. Yeah.

In April, Henry P. Whitehouse was going to be prosecuted by the United States Justice Department for the illegal distribution of the drug MRX2857. The prosecution wasn't revealing many details of their case. However, I was told Charles David Buffalo's involvement was being investigated. And if, in fact, Charles David Buffalo had enabled Whitehouse, then his Last Will and Testament would be revoked on the grounds that his wishes put me in a harmful and unlawful situation. A lawyer from the prosecution had hinted to me one day, as we were going over my testimony, that they "had them both." I assumed this meant Whitehouse and CDB were going down together. I found this strange because one of them was dead.

"Can you prosecute a man's bones?" I asked the lawyer.

The man responded with a smile, "Only his legacy, brother."

The case had become somewhat of a national interest. The United States Department of Justice had decided to hold the trial locally at the downtown courthouse. The Tired Coast was not used to seeing this kind of attention; neither was I. Reporters stretched around the outside of the Buffalo estate from dawn to dusk. They looked like zombies and very well could have been. They reached their arms through the gates and clawed in my direction as I wheeled my bicycle from the garage.

A popular story spreading around the news outlets at the time was that Whitehouse had prescribed MRX2857 to other patients as well. Some claimed these patients had been in Bush's "War-On-Terror." I had hoped this was not true.

"James," I remember one reporter asking in a deep voice, "if Doctor Whitehouse did prescribe other patients MRX2857, would you be willing to meet with them?"

"Yes, we could all play tennis or something," I said. I then got on my bike and flew down the hill leading up to the estate as the media raced behind me in their vans. They followed me as I tucked around the winding curves of the road. In the city they were met with traffic and I was able to drift peacefully away in the bike lane.

Later in the afternoon, when I returned from my ride, I noticed the reporters were still outside. Annoyed, I circled around the front of the estate and climbed a large pine tree. I started throwing pinecones at the men and women near the front gate. They scattered behind their vans. A few of them left. Most stayed.

I climbed down from the tree and decided to swim some laps in the pool. I then took some time to myself in the estate's gardens. My anger began to fade, and my sadness started to dissolve into something manageable.

I had been thinking about my final days at Saint Victoria's Medical Hospital often as the trial approached. I hadn't told anyone about the dreams. I was afraid I would be asked to recount them in court, or in front of a camera. Truthfully, I just wanted all the attention I was receiving to go away.

I made an effort to tame the estate's overgrown plant life upon my return. I tackled the reeds first. The grass in the back was not as tall as I had dreamt, though reducing its size was no easy feat. After a few weeks with a weed-whacker, I was able to run a mower through the grass, creating something that resembled a lawn. I slept a lot better at night after working in the yard.

One afternoon around sunset, it became clear that the reporters were not going to go away until the trial was over. I watched them, as they watched me working in the gardens. It occurred to me as I finished trimming some shrubs that the people outside the gate were just trying to make a living. I went upstairs and showered. Afterward I changed into my robe and had a few drinks. I watched from my bedroom as the people huddled together outside. It got cold once the Sun disappeared beneath the bluffs. The men and women had pulled jackets out from their vans. I noticed a few of them were laughing as they talked amongst themselves. I walked downstairs and lit the fireplace in the living room. I fiddled with the buffalo necklace around my neck and felt incredibly alone.

The next morning, I decided to open up a bit before going on my morning ride. I let one of those reporters I had scared off back onto the estate for a quick one-to-one. He had his crew do a "once-around" the property to make sure all the stray pinecones were moved out of my reach. I agreed to do a short television interview promoting the reprinting of *The Seven Dreams*. The public's interest in the novel had sparked once I became a spectacle. I had to bite my tongue when the reporter closed the exclusive with "James Buffalo, he can write! Who knew?"

I didn't say much during the piece, which only lasted fifty-five seconds. I was pretty absent-minded the entire interview, as I stared past the reporter into the vastness of the Pacific Ocean, and did not speak coherently until the final ten seconds, in which I turned straight into the camera and said, "Mary Ann, please come back."

CHAPTER
— 28 —

In April, Henry P. Whitehouse pleaded guilty to the distribution of an illegal substance. His legal team folded like assembly chairs beneath the weight of the United States Department of Justice. Eli and my pale friend, Dr. Weston Flank, delivered testimonies detailing my collapse. Of course, I took the stand as well. When it was over, Eli and Wes triumphantly burst through the court doors, clapping their hands as two policemen escorted Doctor Whitehouse through the back of the courtroom. "We did it, James," Wes said once we were outside. I looked around as a wave of reporters pushed toward us. "We did something..." I replied as I slid into a town car. Thankfully, Lucia was more than willing to answer questions on my behalf for the tired-looking reporters who had gathered outside the courthouse like ants on sugar.

There was not much of a defense for Doctor Whitehouse. He had blabbed like the coward I had always wanted him to be. And more important, he gave up the deceased Charles David Buffalo, rendering the "deceased's Last Will and Testament void." The inheritance was mine. Whitehouse described to the judge how CDB had shipped large amounts of the drug out of the Congo before his death. He had disguised the drug as a generic heart medicine. And he told the truth. The cops found a "substantial amount" of MRX2857 still left at his apartment. They also found old letters in which Charles David Buffalo instructed him to prescribe me the drug. It was scary to think months earlier, if things had not changed, I would have swallowed every last pill in that apartment. When they asked Whitehouse why he didn't stop administering the drug after Charles David Buffalo died, he looked up into the prosecutor's eyes, and with full certainty he said, "Because James was unwell."

The prosecution was scheduled to hold a press conference an hour after the deliberation. Amidst the circus, I was nowhere to be found, causing some frustration among the media, as the show's main attraction had gone astray. The town car had dropped me off at the estate, and I wasted no time stretching out in the grass, at the edge of the West Wing's bluff, my eyes shining like diamonds.

Lucia had no problem with the attention I loathed. She had perfected the art of seamlessly transitioning and bending the questions regarding my absence into cross-promotions of her new, futuristic French fashion boutique, fittingly called "Lucia."

"What am I wearing, you ask? Well... oh, where's James? Um, he couldn't make it. I'm wearing *Lucia*, by the way." And she would giggle.

She and Eli had spent all of February and March in France before the opening hearings started and surprisingly had managed to stay together. They seemed happy, and for that, my blessing was theirs. It all seemed rather comical, as I pictured Lucia answering the reporters' questions outside the courthouse with an ease I could never understand. They would ask, "Lucia, can you comment on how this transfer of wealth will affect James's life?"

"Well, James is very *laissez-faire* when it comes to things like that," she would say. "It's why we all love him so much. He's very French in a way. I found a great deal of inspiration in the aristocratic French sectors."

And Lucia would go on to answer questions in that manner.

I was just relieved that the attention was slowly coming off of me. Peacefully alone, I found some love, once again, lying on my stomach. I raised my hands above my head and watched as Doris's ashes streamed and spiraled in the coastal wind and sailed across the morning ocean. I could taste her moving spirit, my heart beating like a million happy drums as her dust climbed the western breeze, caught wind drifts off the cliffs that pushed her out to sea. For an instant, I felt that sort of fixed feeling that I had longed for. I have an understanding that no one is ever as fixed as they would like to be.

Crash, crash, the Pacific roared throughout the day.

"What's that?" I bellowed from above as the last of Doris's ashes dispersed and disappeared, like a vanishing swarm of lovely bees.

Crash, crash, replied the Pacific.

"Answer me!" I screamed.

Crash, crash, answered the Pacific.

"We can't hear you up here!"

Crash, crash, you fool! The Pacific roared again, pounding its cold fists against the bluffs.

"Do that again!" I demanded.

Crash, crash.

"Take care of Doris," I begged.

Crash, crash, the ocean frothily rapped.

And in that instant, I felt as though I understood everything a little more. Before, after, during, and at that moment, it was all *crash, crash,* and it was all wonderfully the same. There was nothing left to do but smile, so I put my coffee-stained teeth to the Sun with my palms open. I could feel Doris's soft hand in mine as I waited for that next set to hit the bluffs.

"Is that you, Doris?"

I listened and heard *crash, crash,* and a familiar bird started to sing from his home burrowed in the bluffs, *chirp, chirp,* so I kept my palms up in the warm Sun, feeling her touch. I laughed as the wind blew grass that tickled my kneecaps, and I sat still as the wind blew hair that tickled my brow. I screamed with delight as the wind blew across the ocean—making waves that were destined to say, *crash, crash*.

In the Sun of a good day, I said both hello and good-bye to Doris. Atop the bluffs, I felt the most wonderful sensation as I contemplated an everlasting existence.

It had occurred to me that I was doing a fine job of whatever it is I should be doing. *Yes, I was going to keep going*, I thought. And I knew moments of clarity, like the one I was experiencing, would eventually fade and I would be filled with suffering once again. However, I was learning to trust myself as I made uncomfortable transitions. So, with nothing but an empty urn patterned with purple lavender flowers in my hands, uncertainty, and returning angst, I was ready to pack up and leave the Tired Coast for a bit, looking to move across the Rocky Mountain range.

I had received an invitation from an independent publisher in Denver. They wanted three hundred pages of my soul in exchange for room and board. It was not the best financial offer I had received to write; however, it was a good fit, and I wasn't really struggling for money at the moment. I was more than ready to pick up the pen in Denver, salivating at the possible start of something new. The editor was convinced I still had enough heartbreak in me to write another best seller. Yes, by then *The Seven Dreams* was that popular. My next novel was sure to kill, he said, as it was to be a love story about modern pills, the mind, the everlasting Dharma, and, of course, a great woman. *Laughs all around.*

In the last week of April, I received the official court documents voiding CDB's Last Will and Testament. I was eager to leave for Denver. I would take Doris with me, of course. When I got scared and nervous, sad and alone, I would turn my hands, palms to the Sun, and she would always be there to hold my hand.

Doris would always live in my love for the West, and she would always have a place to dance in my beating heart. I would make her proud, with my head held high. I could feel her above me, perhaps in the clouds, up where the tiny bluebirds make good love. With her up there, how I could I ever curse the heavens?

On the day of my departure, a light rain was falling when I awoke somewhat excitedly in the still morning. I packed up all my necessary belongings, mainly rags of clothes, a bus ticket to Denver, and a laptop computer I had purchased a few weeks back. I shoved everything into my old pack and put it at the foot of my bed. I looked out over the estate, watching the soft rain fall throughout the gardens.

My beard was long, the grass was clean, and the roses cut and trimmed. I had spent most of April tending to the estate's gardens. Along the walls of my room, I had posted clippings depicting various things, such as

"How to Properly Plant a Bulb" or "Shrubs for Early Season Color." I would miss the escape of digging into the soft soil and smelling the scent that arises from tending to paper-thin rosebuds.

I sat on the edge of my bed watching the rain until eventually it was time to say good-bye to Lucia and Eli. Though I doubted their interest, I promised to send them some short stories once the stories were published in the spring. Still, they promised to visit, and I had to listen to Lucia rant on and on about all the Rockies players she thought were "adorable," while Eli paced about and scoffed at the mention of each ballplayer's name. Lucia's previous boyfriend had been a ballplayer.

CHAPTER
— 29 —

Stepping out into the rain, too eager to wait for the taxi I had scheduled, I walked straight into town without looking back. I had dropped my bike off at the UPS Store the day before, and it was already being shipped to my publisher's office in Denver. Eli had told me he had seen Charlie down by Peterson's again, so I was determined to meet him before my bus took off later in the afternoon. I needed to go to the bank as well, so I had Eli write some directions on a napkin, which I had pocketed.

Eventually, I found myself rounding the familiar curves of Market Street. As I turned the corner of Elm, I saw a small mob of people huddled underneath Peterson's Liquor, its sign not yet lit up but not completely dead in the grey lunchtime sky, its letters aglow with the faintest of pinks. I crossed the street and went over to the storefront, where a group of street bums were outside drinking a few light beers from tall, dark cans. I quickly recognized the man I had come to see, the heartbeat of all the Western bums, all wrapped up in conspiracy and simple tyranny. Yes, I was happy to see my old friend Charlie back outside Peterson's.

"James Buffalo!" he yelled as I approached the group.

"How are you, Charlie?" I asked as he rushed to grab my hand and take me into a warm embrace.

"I am on top of it all!" he shouted and wrapped his arms around my back, which normally would have been unpleasant, given his bathing habits, but he appeared clean in a slightly tattered blue suit.

"I worried about you this winter. Awfully cold, even for an old sage like you," I said looking him over once.

Charlie shrugged. "I was up in Santa Barbara. Now dats cold, mah man." His blue eyes lit up. "James Buffalo!" he screamed again and burst into laughter, nodding his head up and down for a minute or so, eventually losing his steam and straightening out all rigid and upright as if he had forgotten what was so funny. So we stood in a few seconds of strange silence, then he started to question me, poking a finger into my canvas pack. "Been back for months now, where's was chu?" he demanded.

"Oh, I have been running around, Charlie." Somehow he had managed to miss the news about the trial entirely.

"You got a girl?" he said, eyeing my beard.

"Uh, no," I replied.

"Hey, did you know they think you wrote a book, James? Goddamn *Seven Queens* it's called. I saw it on a window!"

"Yeah, uh, it's called *The Seven*—"

Charlie interrupted me as he once again hopped another train of thought. "You going on a trip?" he said, nudging my boots with his dirty sneakers.

I laughed. "I am I going to Denver, Charlie. Here, I have a surprise for you. Stop busting my balls." I had stowed a bottle of wine in my backpack. I handed it to him, but he simply brushed it aside, being as difficult as ever.

"Ha," he shouted, waving his thermos. "Just tea for me!" And I could tell Charlie was doing better; I could tell he had taken the leap. When I got to Denver I was going to work on that tea thing myself, though big cities were tough to stay dry in. "Hey, der is someone I wantch yuw ta meet before you goh." He motioned toward the load on my back. "Follow me!" he yelled. With a jerk, he pulled my arm and dragged me down a few blocks past San Pedro Avenue. We got to talking about his sobriety and my upcoming trip to the Rockies. Charlie even went as far as to admit that he had never actually been in the band Edward Sharpe and the Magnetic Zeros. And he told me he no longer had any angst for politicians because they were just poorly operated, or broken puppets. He couldn't decide which. He may have been getting "right," but he was still wonderfully mad, and we both knew that. After a few blocks, caught in conversation, we almost walked past our destination, and we had to walk a few paces back to pause outside of a health-food store named

Wheat's. Charlie pressed his face against the window, which was covered in decorative spring paint (a bushel of yellow apples), and I did the same.

"Ya' see her?" he said as I peered inward and eyed a tall, busty redhead in line at the fast checkout. "Not her!" Charlie said and slapped me in the back of my head. "Her! Ain't she beautiful?" He pointed again, this time at a store clerk who was carrying a satchel of oranges across the floor toward the produce aisle. She was an older brunette with her hair tied up in a bun and a nose slender and pretty. She looked like she was of some European descent, possibly Italian. Her left arm was covered in a bright tattoo sleeve highlighted by a grip of jumping fishes of all different colors. I couldn't make out the rest of the design, though Charlie led me to believe it led to more secretive places. Her face was wrinkled and soft like comfortable leather, and she had a tiny nose ring that moved about when she smiled at the customers. "Uh-huh! She's mine!" exclaimed Charlie, proud as ever. He tapped lightly on the glass to catch her attention.

I was skeptical, but the clerk blushed and giggled, and I could tell that she really was Charlie's. I watched the wrinkles on her face dance as she smiled and her face turned a darker red. She waved for Charlie to get gone.

"That's great, Charlie," I said, and I really meant it.

"Her name is Gloria!" he said and beamed as the old yet still-pretty clerk pointed up to the clock and held up six fingers.

"I get off at six," she mouthed.

Charlie grinned at me and I bowed my head in approval. Charlie had met Gloria Pampanelli while he was in Santa Barbara that winter. It turned out that he went up there for some sort of state-administered alcohol rehabilitation program. Might have been part of the reason he no longer had as much angst for the government. The program had given him love and a clean mind.

No clutter, I thought.

Charlie interrupted my daydreaming with some wonderful news. "We gettin' married next week!" he shouted and flashed a huge smile. Gloria waved in my direction, and I could in fact see the glimmer of a modest diamond on her finger. "Took me three weeks celery, workin' at duh Sal Army. You know, the one dawn the street. I figure I know everrrone there already, middas well keep a job now that I've got a reason to. Hell..." He grabbed me by the strap on my back and pulled me in real close. "I want to give her the world, James."

"Charlie, you dog," I said as I wrapped my arm around his shoulder.

He started to cry tears of joy, turning away from the window and lifting his head up toward the grey sky, which was crying, too. And after a while, the two of us just standing there in the rain, I asked Charlie if

I could try on his jacket. He laughed, wiping the tears and rain away from his face. I took off my pack and slid the blue jacket on over my white T-shirt, making sure to button the tiny brown rivets all the way up to my neck. The jacket didn't fit my skinny frame very well, and the sleeves were too long. Still, I liked the way it hung off my arms and the way my fingers barely escaped from its cuffs, like a fox sticking his nose out of a burrow.

"You can have it, if you like," Charlie selflessly offered, even as he was becoming drenched, exposed in his own stained undershirt.

"No," I said as I looked at my reflection in a moving street puddle. "No, it looks much better on you."

"Bah!" He shook his head as I handed back the coat.

"I just need these boots here, and my pack," I said.

"I see," he said looking upset. "You ain't cumin to the weddin', are ya?"

"Afraid not, Charlie." I knew I couldn't come back home to the Tired Coast without feeling some sort of sadness or lament, at least not for a while.

"Welp," he said, looking at me. "Can I do your honors?"

"Charlie—" I started, ready to explain myself.

He cut me off. "You're getting married, too, James."

"I am?" I said.

"Yes." Charlie nodded and pulled a pack of cigarettes from his back pocket, removing one stick dramatically as if were a great sword. "To the *West*, James." He smiled and handed me the cigarette, trying to keep a straight face. "And this, my good friend, is God's cigarette." He bowed down and handed me the cigarette, losing his footing and landing ass first in an oil-slicked puddle. I tried to help him up, and I lost my footing as well, joining him on the wet asphalt. "To the West!" he shouted. And with that, we both busted up real good, because Charlie had just said the funniest thing either of us had ever heard. Turning toward the south part of town where the city bus stopped the most, I got up and hugged Charlie. And all that I could think to tell him was, *Good job keep going.* I'm not sure why, but it seemed like the right thing to say, and old Charlie just stood there smiling, not saying a word, shaking his head, before pressing his face back against the glass to watch his love work.

I still needed to go to the bank, so I pulled Eli's directions from my front pocket. The falling rain and afternoon puddle hopping with Charlie had smeared the ink across the napkin, and I was left trying to decide whether I needed to make a Louie or a Richard, when I heard shouting coming from the Wheat's parking lot. I turned around and saw Charlie being dragged away from the storefront as Gloria screamed at a couple of cops who had Charlie in their grasp.

"I told you, you're smearing the goddamn window with your stink!" one of them said. The other chimed in with, "You fucking bum."

I would find out later that Gloria's ex-husband had been a cop. An ex-alcoholic himself, Jackson Pampanelli had been the one who suggested Gloria go to Santa Barbara for treatment. He had no idea that his wife would return sober with divorce papers and distaste for him. Jackson was furious at Gloria's betrayal. He was not a bad man, and he was a decent husband. Gloria just couldn't be around him anymore for reasons she never wanted to explain. She loved Charlie, and it was killing the ex-cop to know that a man who declared his only true residence to be beneath the stars had displaced him. Jackson's buddies had been giving the pair a difficult time ever since it was known the two of them were engaged. So the cops smiled and shoved Charlie back and forth.

"Let's count here, Chuck," suggested the young lieutenant named Earl Robertson.

"One, two," the other cop, Jack Taylor, said.

"Yep, that's right, Taylor. One, two, and here we are at three. It looks like we get to take you in for being a public asshole, Charlie. That's the third time this week the owner has complained about you smudging the window."

"That's not true!" yelled Gloria.

"Honestly, bro, I don't even want to put him in the back of our car," said Taylor to Robertson. "He smells like tuna fish."

The two cops started laughing hysterically as they shoved an embarrassed Charlie into the back of the cop car. Gloria walked up to the window and tried to console Charlie, but he was too sad to even look up. She was used to the routine, and she had begged Charlie to stay away from the store. But he just couldn't help it. Frozen across the intersection, I watched as Gloria turned toward the cops. With her wrinkled face tight and rigid, she issued some heavy yet ultimately empty threats. There was really nothing she could do. People in that town were programmed to like a bad cop like Jackson more than a bum like Charlie.

CHAPTER
— 30 —

After a few frantic wrong turns, completely winded and soaking wet, I found myself outside the bank where my money had recently been transferred. I wasted no time in requesting that ten percent of the money I had access to be transferred into a safe deposit box. I wanted the key. That's right. I asked them to put two hundred and eighty-five thousand dollars in a safe deposit box. "Now!" I shouted, thinking about those twisted fucks Robertson and Taylor.

I was causing quite a stink, or maybe a stir, in the bank. A group of employees came over to examine my credentials and examine my proof of identity, as large money always brings about small questions. Sadly, all I had to my name at the moment was a crumpled passport and my tired eyes. So of course I caught some flak as they asked me "my mother's maiden name" and "the last four digits of my Social Security number." Big money— small questions. Everyone in the place was looking me up and down with disbelief and bitterness, eyeing my pack and my ragged beard. I shuffled my boots with a squeak on the tile floor and felt awkward asking for *my money*!

"Planning a trip?" questioned the cute Asian clerk.

I just stared at her, not saying a word.

"And, Mr. Buffalo, would you like to list someone as a beneficiary of the safe deposit box in case you cannot access it?" she asked without looking up from her computer. *Tap. Tap. Tap.*

"Oh, of course. This box isn't for me. I want to leave it for a friend," I said as I scribbled a name on the back of an informational credit-building pamphlet. I shoved the handout across the counter.

"Okay," she said. "I'll add her as a beneficiary. You will still be able to access this if you change your mind." She continued to punch away on her keyboard before turning the screen in my direction and, with a cupped hand so only my eyes could see, she asked, "Did I spell the name right?"

"Yes, I think so," I replied, feeling more and more awkward as eyes turned toward me from all directions. I nodded toward the people staring at me. "Real strange cats around here," I said to the girl.

"But why are you so surprised?" She sighed and leaned on the counter, placing a hand on her forehead and lowering her voice. "People are so peculiar in this town." I could tell then that the little clerk had tired eyes, too, as she glanced around at her coworkers, who were turning to whispers and envy at the handling of such a large transaction.

"It will take a day or so to deposit the money in the box, you know." She brushed a thin strand of black hair away from her face, and it grazed her tiny nose.

"As quickly as possible," I replied, tapping my fingers on the marble.

"Of course," she said.

After a few slow minutes and a few more security procedures, she slid a tiny key into a tiny envelope labeled 1978B and handed it across the counter as her coworkers shot me dead looks of jealousy. "The key won't be good enough on its own. You or the other person will have to show some identification."

The little Asian clerk, whose name tag read "Rachel," seemed depressed, and I thought I understood why. When I left, her manager would probably chew her out for not chatting me up some more. *A high-priority customer,* he would scream as I left the bank, *and you can't at least muster a little more charisma, Rachel!* I felt bad because I knew Rachel would just look up with her tired eyes and not say a word. I wanted to tell her it was all just a sham, but I said nothing.

I had turned on the tile flooring and headed for the door when suddenly one of the elder bank managers grabbed my arm. "Listen," I said. "I have all the right paperwork. Just let me be!" Then I noticed that he had a copy of *The Seven Dreams* in his hand.

"Here," he said. "Will you sign this for me?"

I said I would but that I needed a favor in return. "Can you take this envelope to Wheat's?" I asked. "Ask for a lady named Gloria." The man looked at me. I could tell he was good man.

"For you it would be an honor, James," replied the bank manager as he shook my hand firmly. My bus was set to arrive in less than half an hour, and the next one wasn't due until the following morning. The thought of spending another day in that town was giving me the chills, so I thanked the man and left as quickly as I could. Farther down, toward the south end of Market Street, I felt a little relieved as I realized I was closer to my destination than I previously imagined, my stop visible across the park.

I need to get out more once I'm in Denver, I thought.

I sat down on the park bench where I had sat with Mary Ann Lewis on an equally rainy day in December. I felt compelled to smoke the cigarette Charlie had given me when he declared my marriage to the West. I remembered how Mary Ann Lewis had told me about Jesus Christ; I remembered thinking that she was so far gone in the Dharma she didn't even realize it. I really missed her. And then I felt a little depressed as I remembered how I felt when Mary Ann Lewis told me about the doctors she worked for and all the bad secrets she'd learned while walking the seventh-floor halls, I, ignorant and oblivious to it all, drinking warm tea a few floors above. And I remembered how I told her I wasn't sure Doctor Henry Whitehouse was hiding anything, and I remembered how she had laughed under her bright-red umbrella. I had come to understand what she had meant when she said Doctor Whitehouse was in fact hiding me. I didn't then, but as I finished my cig and planted it in the nearest ashtray, I understood perfectly.

Heaving my pack over my shoulders, I headed across the park's muddy grass toward the bus stop, which was located near Doctor Henry P. Whitehouse's recently vacated corner office. I wanted to see the place one last time before I left. I rounded the familiar corner of Elm Street, and I started to laugh as the rain began to fall harder and harder, my hair plastered down over my eyes. I thought about Charlie again, and I smiled, picturing his face when Gloria showed up at the police station to tell him that their troubles were all over. The bank manager was probably arriving at Wheat's at that moment to deliver the key for Charlie's bail money and then some. Charlie and Gloria were going to have a very nice and a very beautiful wedding, hopefully somewhere outside of the Tired Coast, where Jackson and his boys couldn't reach them.

For the first time in a while I felt really good, and I could care less about the money. I just wanted enough to live and love. Charlie could have his Mary Ann Lewis, and that made me feel at peace. I just wanted to take that leap as I strolled underneath Doctor Henry P. Whitehouse's old office. Truth be told, big wealth in America scared me. I was afraid of what it might turn me into. I was afraid what it might keep me from doing.

Yes, I needed to stay desperate in America. I needed to sharpen my teeth on her sidewalks, toughen myself on her streets, before biting into her fleshy heart, and, most important, I needed to dirty my palms and boots in the soot of a big city before bathing in her great blue springs. I was ready to leave.

On the street below the Doctor's office, the tall street lamps started to spring to life as the sky got darker. I thought I could see a dim light on the eleventh floor do the same, and I was certain I could hear the teapot's cry, like a sick bird. I felt sorry for whoever was up in that building. So, I pushed my boots forward, humming to myself, my head filled with the stars of possibility. I splashed my way across the street and rounded the corner, eventually stopping underneath the northbound bus stop overhang, wishing I had another cigarette, waiting for the five-thirty bus to arrive. I was going to make my own wonderfully meager living doing what I pleased, as free as flower petals moving about in the warm western winds. Maybe someday, I could come back to the Tired Coast on my own terms, but then again, maybe not.

It was just about time for my bus to arrive, and I lifted my head from a Colorado state map I had bought. I looked across the street toward the old building for what I assumed to be the last time. As I did, a tiny black cat scampered off the sidewalk and down the alleyway. I followed the cat with my eyes as far as I could down the slim urban crevice before it eventually disappeared. Bringing my eyes back out of the darkness, I noticed a large mural painted on the alley's brick wall, adjacent to the Doctor's office building. It was partly hidden behind a decaying Dumpster and cardboard suburbia. From what I could see of the mural, there appeared to be a beautiful beach painted on the red brick—quite a contradiction to the surrounding grime and falling rain.

Curiosity got the cat.

I crossed the street, taking the same path the feline had taken, to get a better view of the mural. An old airplane was streaming through a blue-painted sky. And along a sand-covered beach, a tiny adobe city stretched itself across the brick coastline. I could make out what looked like tiny people in bright costumes dancing in the streets and tiny fruit carts appeared to be posted up in the shade of a few storefront overhangs, depicting a town full of both life and celebration. I pushed my hands against the cold wet bricks, stepped back, and turned my head up into the heavy rain to take it all in. I studied the mural, and I noticed red letters painted at the bottom just underneath the painted beach, partly obscured by oversized black trash bags. I tossed the bags aside and read the faded lettering:

Puerto Avion, Mexico

Mexico, I thought, and looked up at the vibrant city scene as the rain fell harder and harder, the street lamps growing brighter, shining down on the hidden city, my heart racing. I was instantly taken back to the conversation I had with Eli on the side of Highway 101 in Los Angeles. "She said something about Mexico..." Eli's words echoed in my head, "...she was obviously lying."

No. I couldn't help but imagine Mary Ann Lewis had meant for me to find this mural. Perhaps she thought I would crack and return to Doctor Henry P. Whitehouse, and perhaps she thought this mural would call me away from the Tired Coast and its many modern pills. So, after a few more minutes, I shuffled back out of the alley and into the street, where I stopped a nurse who had just finished her shift and was walking toward her car in the back lot.

"Excuse me, Miss," I said, pointing back down the alleyway toward the fading paint on the red bricks. "How long has this been here?"

The chubby young blonde, her short hair curled by the rain, looked up at the painting and smiled. "Before someone built another building in front of it." She nodded toward the conveniently located Walgreens.

"Of course," I replied. And when she left, I pulled my tiny buffalo necklace from under my soaked T-shirt. *Puerto Avion, Mexico*, I thought as I ran my fingers across the engraved *P.A.*

As I stood in thought, the little black cat came back out of the alley from underneath one of the Dumpsters, arching his back, rubbing himself against my leg, and wrapping his tail around one of my ankles. I wanted to thank him, so I leaned over to protect him from the rain.

Looking at his green eyes, I noticed that he was not a stray after all. His tiny collar glimmered in the dim light.

"Did you want me to see this, buddy?" I said to the little cat. I reached down and turned the collar to see what I should call him, and I had another good laugh as I saw that *he* was in fact a *she*, and her plated name tag read:

DHARMA

I laughed and then cried for a bit, smothered in the irony. A black cat named *Dharma*. Possibly leading me back to Mary Ann Lewis. How fitting. So I held the cat tight as long as I could before she eventually jumped out of my arms and disappeared into the darkness of the alleyway. In the heavy rain, I leaned back against the red brick and screamed for everyone to hear, "DHARMA'S A HOUSE CAT," and I laughed and laughed. With a hand on the strap of my pack, I walked back across the street and sat down under the southbound overhang, listening to the rain steadily drumming on the plastic cover, thinking deeply about a black cat named Dharma, thinking deeply of Mary Ann Lewis, and waiting, just waiting, for the next bus to Mexico.

As I said from the beginning, by all means,
this is a love story.